LOVE
REDEFINED

AMANDA WRAY

FORT COLLINS, COLORADO

Publishing House
Sioux Ink
2156 Ballard Lane
Fort Collins, Colorado 80524
www.siouxink.com

Love Redefined: A Lesbian Romance Novel / Amanda Wray -- 1st ed.
Paperback ISBN-13: 978-1-946317-06-3
ISBN-1 0: 1-946317-06-3

DEDICATION

I dedicate this book to my loving wife, Stacy.
She has supported me through this entire process, believ-
ing in me, even when I didn't believe in myself.

GET EXCLUSIVE ACCESS TO

AMANDA WRAY'S NEXT NOVEL

HTTPS://MAILCHI.MP/60D2B6EC0337/AMANDAWRAY

~1~

I can't believe I have to waste my whole day at the fucking DMV, Lisa thought.

She had been there for nearly an hour, standing in about the same spot the entire time.

I have to pee like a mad woman. This thought was urgent.

She turned to the woman standing behind her, a beautiful woman in her late 20s—long black hair, ivory skin, deep brown eyes, and a smile that made you smile right back.

"I hate to ask, but would you hold my place in line? I have got to get to the bathroom before I explode," Lisa said with a look of desperation on her face.

"Sure, no problem," the stunning woman replied.

Grateful, Lisa ran to the bathroom. When she returned, she thanked the woman; for the first time she noticed her immense beauty.

"I'm sorry, I didn't even ask your name. I'm not usually this rude, I promise."

"It's okay; this place tends to bring out the worst in people. My name is Katrina. What're you in for?" She looked at Lisa with a coy smile.

"I let my registration lapse. What an idiot, huh? I didn't realize until I got pulled over. I guess I've been a little too busy to notice."

Lisa was grateful to have someone to talk to in this God-forsaken place. The pair spent the next two hours talking and laughing, like they had known each other their whole lives. When it was almost Lisa's turn, she decided that she was going to do something she would never normally do. But, she felt confident. *We really connected, right?*

"Would you like to go to lunch sometime?" she blurted. *Goddamn it! You're such an idiot! Real smooth, dumbass!* She cursed herself.

Katrina's eyes flashed with what Lisa hoped was excitement. "Absolutely! How about after we get out of this hellhole? I'm free 'til two."

"That sounds perfect," Lisa said, trying to keep her cool. "I'll meet you outside in a few minutes then."

Lisa felt like she was floating. Now she was glad she had let her registration lapse. When she was finished, she looked over her shoulder; Katrina had just made it up to the window to renew her license.

Lisa quickly ducked into the restroom again. She didn't have to pee this time; she had to make sure she looked *good*.

She gazed at her reflection. Short, blonde hair, a little tussled. She ran her fingers through it a few times. *Check to make sure I don't have anything disgusting stuck in my teeth*, she thought as she bared her teeth, gave her plump pink lips a swipe of chap-stick, then stood back to admire herself. *Damn, I look good.* She smiled and flew out of the lady's room.

Lisa stood outside for about fifteen minutes waiting for Katrina, getting more nervous with each passing minute. *I wish I still smoked*, she thought, trying to calm herself.

As Katrina walked out the double doors Lisa took a deep breath in a futile attempt to stop her hands from shaking. She couldn't help but smile.

Under the fluorescent lighting of the DMV, Katrina was stunning in the sunlight, she was like a sun-kissed Goddess. The sun brought out the amber highlights in her hair and the golden flakes in her eyes.

For a moment Lisa forgot how to breathe altogether. When Katrina reached her she realized she had been holding her breath, she let it all out at once.

"Wow, sorry. I just noticed your eyes."

Fuck, now I sound like an idiot. This girl probably thinks I'm a freak. She's never going to talk to me again. She's probably going to come up with an excuse to not have lunch with me too. Idiot!

"Thank you; your eyes are like the ocean, that deep blue," Katrina returned the compliment, her cheeks turning slightly pink.

"Well, now that we got that out of the way, where would you like to go to lunch? What sounds good to you?"

"You know, I have been dying to try that new place right around the corner. What's it called, 'The Taste of Love?'"

"Me too! Yeah, we can walk there. It's the perfect day for a walk."

They walked along talking about the weather, their favorite foods, nothing much in general. Lisa was in awe of how easily the conversation flowed. Through lunch, there was never much of a lag in conversation, except of course when they were shoving food in their mouths.

"This is the most amazing food," Katrina gushed with a mouthful of pasta.

"I think I found my new favorite restaurant," Lisa agreed.

"And a new favorite person to come here with," Katrina smiled, flirting a little.

Lisa couldn't help but smile back. This was possibly the most amazing woman she had ever met. They had so much in common, and she had never felt so comfortable with anyone before.

"So, I guess the only thing we haven't talked about is relationship status." Lisa tried to sound nonchalant but didn't think she really succeeded.

"I'm completely single. I'm very picky, I guess. The last guy I dated turned out to be a real sleaze ball, that was over a year ago. It took me a long time to get over that," Katrina replied. "What about you?"

Shit, she's straight. "I just recently broke up with my longtime girlfriend. She was more interested in partying than spending time on our relationship. I guess I was kind of fucked up for a while too." Lisa blushed, thinking she had probably revealed too much.

"I'm so sorry." Katrina looked into her eyes with what felt like genuine compassion. "Things always happen for a reason. I know that sounds really cliché, but it's true. If I hadn't been through that mess with Brock, I would have never moved to Denver. I wouldn't have had to get a new Colorado driver's license, and I would have never met you. I would have never had the most amazing bowl of pasta I have ever tasted," she said with a smile.

Lisa couldn't help but laugh. "That's very true. It was completely by chance that I chose today to go to the DMV. I put it off for as long as possible. I finally made myself go. I guess it was destiny, right?" She felt her cheeks get hot.

"Definitely. Damn it; it's already 1:30. We'd better head back to the parking lot."

"I guess you're right. I think I need to walk so my stomach doesn't feel like it's going to explode."

Lisa left a tip on the table for the waitress; she was so absorbed in Katrina, she hadn't even noticed her. They walked back to their cars; it didn't seem to take long enough.

"I had a great time with you today. The best trip I have ever made to the DMV. We should do this again sometime—minus the DMV." Katrina seemed to glow as she spoke. Maybe it was the sunlight on this gorgeous July day, maybe it was Lisa's imagination, maybe she was feeling the same thing Lisa was.

"Absolutely, let me give you my number. You can call me or text me whenever. I pretty much have my phone on me all the time, except when I'm in the shower."

"Good to know." Katrina smiled her mind-numbing smile. "I'll give you a buzz soon. Next time it's my treat." She reached up and gave Lisa a warm hug.

Christ, she smells amazing, Lisa thought as she hugged her back. "I'll talk to you soon."

Lisa grinned as she watched Katrina slide into her shiny black Volvo. She didn't walk to her car until the Volvo rounded the corner and was out of sight. She blinked a few times and realized she was standing in the middle of the parking lot with that stupid grin still on her face. She turned and walked quickly to her own vehicle, a yellow Jeep Wrangler with a rag top and huge tires.

She pulled herself up, into the driver's seat, not thinking about what she was doing.

She couldn't take her mind off of Katrina. *I have to text her. No, I can't. I can't seem too eager. She's straight anyway. But, there was something there. I know I wasn't imagining that. I think she felt it too. Damn it, I'm going to do it. It's not too needy; she drove away nine minutes ago. There's no rule, right? No, no; going to wait. Have to wait. Just 'til I get home. That'll be almost an hour. That's long enough.*

She flew home. The drive that normally would have taken an hour took all of 35 minutes.

Well, shit. I can't wait any longer. Now, what to say without being too much of a dork? Here goes nothing.

I had an awesome time @ lunch. Can't wait 2 do it again.

She typed the message into her iPhone, quickly read it over, and hit 'send' before she could chicken out.

The next two minutes were excruciating. Just when she thought she would vomit, her iPhone started to vibrate. She was paralyzed for a moment. She swallowed the huge lump in her throat and looked at the screen. It was a reply from Katrina.

Fuck, fuck, fuck. I am going to throw up. Get it together, dumbass. It's just a text. Just read it.

I had a great time 2. How about dinner tmrw, I'll cook.

Holy shit, Holy shit, Holy shit! Ok, think of something clever to text back. Quickly! If you take too long she's going to know what a lame ass you are.

Lisa quickly texted back.

cool I'll bring the wine

She threw her phone down and ran to the bathroom. After spending some time reliving her lunch, she curled up on the bathroom floor. She realized that her phone was in the other room. Feeling a little sick again, she thought about the text that must be waiting for her. She pulled herself up and washed her mouth out at the sink.

Splashing some water on her face, she took a few deep breaths. *It's okay. She already asked you to dinner. At her place. That's good! But, she's straight, that's bad. Maybe she's not... Damn it! Go check the text already.*

She walked slowly down the hall, holding onto the wall until her vision cleared. She had to search for her phone, which had somehow slid under the couch in her mad dash to the bathroom. She sat on the floor, swallowed hard and clicked on her phone.

That sounds perfect. Cant wait!

Another wave of dizziness hit Lisa. But, this time it was a good thing. *She's excited to see me! I knew there was something. She felt it too. She is the most beautiful person I have ever seen.*

They texted back and forth all day. Every time her phone vibrated, Lisa would get little butterflies. There was definitely something about this girl; she had never fallen for someone this quickly. She tried so hard not to. Her fragile ego couldn't take rejection.

She was so afraid that Katrina was totally straight; that there would be no hope of a future as anything but friends. She tried to see them as just friends. She couldn't. But, she also couldn't see her life without her.

She couldn't imagine not seeing or talking to her every day, which she found incredibly odd because this was the first day she had spent with her, the first day she had known her.

Every time she pictured her flawless face, she felt warmth in her chest.

That night, Lisa couldn't sleep. She was so excited to see Katrina again. She finally drifted off with images of herself and Katrina walking hand-in-hand.

The next day, Lisa woke up before the sun came up. *Damn it. What is wrong with me?* she thought as she rolled out of bed. She had a whole fifteen hours 'til dinner with Katrina. She was going to drive herself crazy until then. *Maybe I should get a haircut. I'm looking a little shaggy.*

She started the coffee pot in her kitchen.She was going to have to keep herself busy today if she was going to make it to dinner without spontaneously combusting.

She retrieved the newspaper left at her door. She decided to read every article in the paper, which would kill a few hours.

She sipped her coffee and turned the pages, not really reading anything. It was incredibly hard to concentrate on anything other than Katrina. Every story reminded Lisa of her, every ad. She was starting to think she was crazy.

Maybe a shower will clear my mind. She took a long hot shower, the whole time thinking how great it would be if Katrina was scrubbing her back. *Aye, how am I going to make it through today? I guess I can go run errands.*

She pulled a blue t-shirt over her blonde head, stepped into her favorite pair of jeans, yanked on her standard white socks and stuck her feet in her jogging shoes. She climbed into her Jeep, plugged in her iPod and started the noisy engine.

She turned up the volume as loud as she could stand, trying to drown out her thoughts. It wasn't working; every song made her think of Katrina. She was going crazy; she was sure of it now.

She stopped at the barbershop. She had gotten her hair cut there for the last five years. She always went to the same girl; Sandy knew some of Lisa's most intimate secrets.

There's something so vulnerable about a person when they allow someone to hold sharp scissors at the back of their head. Lisa smiled as she walked in the door. Sandy was there, and she wasn't busy. Good, Lisa really needed to talk to someone.

"Hey, Chicky! What's going on? You look like hell. Let's fix that wild mane, huh?" Sandy greeted Lisa.

"God, yes! I need some Sandy time," Lisa sighed. They walked back to the sink; she relaxed a bit as Sandy ran her hands through her messy locks. The warm water ran over her tense scalp, relaxing her a little more.

"Alright, hot stuff, tell me what's going on. Why is your scalp so tight?" Sandy inquired.

"There's this girl."

"I see. What's wrong with her? Is she emotionally unavailable? A porn star? A psychopath?

"She's straight," Lisa frowned.

"And you're in love with her." It wasn't a question, more like an observation.

"Yes! I can't get her out of my head! Everything makes me think of her. I can't sleep. My stomach is in knots. I'm going crazy!"

"Tell me about her. What's so special about this girl?"

"Well, she's stunning. She has the most flawless skin I have ever seen, long black hair, brown eyes you can get lost in and the most amazing smile. She's funny, smart and genuine; she's perfect."

"Are you sure she's straight?" Sandy wondered.

"Pretty sure. She talked about her ex-boyfriend at lunch." Lisa frowned again.

"Maybe not; you have an ex-boyfriend, remember."

"True, but that was before I decided it was okay to be gay. Before I embraced my true self."

"Well, maybe she hasn't embraced it yet. Maybe she was just waiting for the right butch-y dyke to come along and sweep her off her feet."

That made Lisa smile a little with hope. "Hmm, that would be amazing. I can't imagine my life without her. I don't know what it is."

"Wow, girl. You have it bad. And we're done." Sandy brushed Lisa's neck and pulled the apron off.

"That's ten for the cut and ten for the advice," Sandy laughed.

"Here's $25; if you're right, it'll be worth it." Lisa hugged Sandy and headed for the door.

"I'll see you in a couple months," Lisa called over her shoulder as she pulled her sunglasses out.

After she climbed back into the Jeep, she pulled her phone out to put it on the charger. She had a missed text.

She immediately got goose bumps. She knew who it was. She opened her phone eagerly.

Cant wait till 2nite. Bring wine. Dinner's @ 7 sharp

Lisa felt her face flush. She might wet herself she was so excited. She text back.

me 2! I'll b early, promise.

She put the Jeep in drive and cranked the volume again. There was no stopping thinking about her now. Lisa couldn't help but smile as she finished her errands.

~2~

Katrina would always remember the moment when she met Lisa. She felt a sizzle that she'd never experienced before.

Since she was ten, Katrina had known she was gay, but she never wanted to let her Christian parents down. She had lived a lie to make them happy, but she was miserable. She wanted to be who she really was.

Stupid DMV, why does it take them so long? I hate this. I can't get cell service here, I don't have anyone to talk to, and I'm starving, Katrina thought as she shifted back and forth on her tired feet.

"I hate to ask, but but would you hold my place in line? I have got to go to the bathroom before I explode," the woman in front of her interrupted her thoughts. She looked so pitiful and desperate; Katrina couldn't help but say yes.

As the woman walked away, Katrina watched her. She was very attractive. Her short blonde hair hanging in her piercing blue eyes, that timid smile. Katrina bit her lip, then quickly looked around to see if anyone was watching.

After the woman got back to the line, Katrina couldn't help but talk to her. She was fascinated by her. And the way she looked at her made her feel all fuzzy inside.

Her stomach growled at the lunch invitation. It was the perfect excuse to spend more time with this gorgeous woman.

Katrina couldn't believe how nervous she was. She had to make sure she looked perfect; she raced for the bathroom.

Ugh! Good thing I always have a brush and extra make-up with me, she thought, scrutinizing herself. She ran the brush through her silky black hair a few quick times, gave her lips a swipe of gloss, and popped a mint in her mouth. *Okay,* she thought, *here goes nothing.* She headed for the door, trying to look confident.

As they walked to the restaurant, Katrina brushed Lisa's hand with hers by accident. The energy sizzled between them. She wanted to just grab it and hold on, but instead pretended like nothing happened.

She had an amazing time at lunch. Lisa was so easy to talk to. She had never connected with anyone like this before. She thought maybe Lisa felt something too; she was sure of it when Lisa asked her if she was seeing anyone.

Katrina wanted to scream at herself when she wouldn't shut up about her ex-boyfriend. She noticed Lisa's smile fade, just a little. She wanted to tell her right then that dating men was a front. She could see herself being with Lisa.

She was having such a great time she'd lost all track of time. She looked at her watch: *damn! I have to be in a meeting in half an hour. I could stay here all day. UGH! If it wasn't mandatory, I would so get out of it.*

While they exchanged phone numbers, Katrina thought her heart was going to beat right out of her chest. She wasn't sure what they said to each other as they stood there, she was too busy watching Lisa's mouth, thinking how amazing it would be to kiss her perfect lips. *I'm just going to do it. I can do this. She's just a human...with an amazing mouth. Who could possibly hate me forever. Or love me forever.*

She reached up, still undecided about what she was going to do. Instead of a kiss, she wrapped her arms around Lisa. It felt so warm, so right. She held on for

16

what was probably a little too long, but Lisa didn't seem to mind.

Finally, she got into her Volvo and drove off, not paying attention to where she was going at all. She could only think about was Lisa. She had to see her again. She had to tell her how she felt. She had never been so scared and so excited at the same time.

She tried to pay attention in her meeting; it was about the big merger her company was working on that was supposed to be completed within a month.

She was the vice president of marketing, so she should've been paying attention. Instead, she was lost in a daydream about kissing Lisa when she felt her phone vibrate. She usually didn't even have her phone with her in meetings, but since she was running a little late today she didn't have time to put it in her office.

Stealthily, she peeked at her phone under the table. *It's Lisa!* She couldn't help but grin. She quickly read the message happily. Her heart was beating in her throat. *She wants to see me again! I have to see her again. Oooh! Tomorrow night, I'll have her over for dinner. I can impress her with my cooking skills.*

She texted back, keeping her phone hidden under the table. She felt like a school girl again. Seconds later her phone was vibrating again. She thought of something witty to text back and hit 'send.' It was a long time before Lisa texted back; Katrina was a little worried she had offended her.

The meeting now over, she was feeling bummed. Walking back to her office, she felt her phone going off again. She walked faster so she could look at it. She plopped into her chair and checked her phone. Sure enough, it was her again! She giggled like a 13 year old; she realized that she wasn't going to be getting any work done this afternoon. She picked up the phone on her desk and dialed her boss.

"Hey Frank, I've got to split. I'll have everything ready by Monday."

"Sure thing. Is everything okay?" Frank asked. He was like a father to Katrina. She could tell him anything, … well, all most anything.

"Everything's cool. I feel like I'm getting a migraine." She felt bad lying, but not being able to stop thinking about someone wasn't a good reason to go home early.

"Alright, kiddo. I'm sure you'll be working hard all weekend on your report. I'll see you bright and early Monday. Don't forget our meeting."

"How could I forget? I'll see you then. Thanks, Frankie." She hung up the phone and threw everything in her bag, almost running for her car.

She had so much to do before tomorrow night. First things first, she needed to clean. This merger had taken so much of her time, her house had suffered. After that, she needed to go shopping for fresh ingredients for her special recipe.

Her mind was going a mile a minute. She couldn't remember the last time she had felt like this. She ran around for the rest of the day trying to get everything done, the whole time texting Lisa. Every time her phone would vibrate she couldn't help but smile.

That night when she went to bed she was exhausted. But, she was also wired. She was so excited about her plans for tomorrow night. *Is it a date?* Katrina wondered as she drifted off to sleep. *Does she think it's a date? I hope everything is perfect.* She dreamed about Lisa all night. All good dreams, about kissing mostly. There was also one about a wedding, which she couldn't quite remember.

She woke early in the morning with a smile on her face. She decided she would go for a jog. *Just a short jog,* she told herself. *Just enough to wake up and get energized.* She ran for about 30 minutes.

When she got home, she headed for the shower. The hot water felt great running down her body. Her legs had felt a little tight after her jog, but now they were relaxed. She spent a long time in the shower just enjoying the sensation of the water slipping down her slender body. When the hot water started to run out she turned off the shower and got out.

She looked at herself in the mirror. She liked what she saw; she worked hard to stay in shape. Her favorite part of her body had to be her shoulders. They were strong but still feminine. She decided that she should show them off tonight.

Her eyes moved down to her breasts. They still looked good, even though she would be 30 next month. Stomach flat, pretty toned actually. Hips, curvy, probably her least favorite part. No matter how many miles she ran they wouldn't get any smaller. She had great legs, runner's legs. Even though she was only 5'4", they were long and strong.

Alright, enough of this. You need to get dressed. She wrapped the towel around her head and headed for the closet. It was only noon, too early to get ready for tonight. So, she threw on a pair of old gray sweats and a black tank top.

She headed to the kitchen to get to work on her dessert. She was making a simple chocolate mousse, but she wanted it to have plenty of time to chill.

She was obsessed with making things perfect. Which was nothing really new for her; you didn't become the VP of marketing before age 30 by being anything but perfect.

She was counting down the hours. At least there were only five hours more to wait.

While she was cleaning up her chocolaty mess, she noticed her phone vibrating across the counter. She was sure it was Lisa, but her hands were covered in chocolate. She quickly finished throwing the dirty dishes into the dishwasher, and then wiped her hands with a paper towel. She grabbed her phone.

what's the address?

Oh god, I didn't even tell her the address, Katrina chastised herself as she texted her address.

on the way, I promised I'd b early.

That made Katrina smile. She wouldn't mind at all.

Well, I guess I better go get dressed so I'm ready when u r.

She could almost see Lisa's face as she read that one.

U better get on it then

Katrina headed to the bathroom to get started. She started with makeup first. She decided to emphasize her eyes. Next, her hair. Since she was cooking, she pulled it back in a simple braid.

Then it was just a matter of picking out the perfect outfit. She searched her closet. She found her red spaghetti strap top and white linen pants. She left her feet bare; it was warm in the house, and it was comfortable to cook barefoot. She was giving herself the once over when her phone started dancing across her dresser.

R u ready?

Katrina looked at the clock, it was nearly four. Lisa was coming three hours early.

Sure, but if ur this early u have 2 help cook

Deal

Katrina was filled with instant butterflies again.

Fifteen minutes later the doorbell rang. *Oh God, don't throw up!*

She calmed herself with a deep breath, then opened the door. There stood Lisa, she looked even better than yesterday.

"You got a haircut. Looks good," Katrina greeted her.

"You look amazing," Lisa gushed. "Your eyes are sparkling." Then she turned the cutest shade of red.

"Well, are you going to come in and help me cook or what?" Katrina smiled and moved aside so Lisa could walk past her.

~3~

She smells even better than yesterday, Lisa thought. She was almost dizzy with the scent of her. She reached down and gave her a quick hug. It felt so good to have her arms around her again. "I brought a red and a white. I wasn't sure what you were making, so I thought one of each was a good idea." She was grinning like an idiot. Katrina was so delightful she couldn't help beaming.

"That's perfect. We can drink the red with dinner and the white after." Katrina couldn't help smiling either. She was in awe that Lisa was in her house right now. "You're going to help me make lasagna."

"Hmm, sounds complicated. But I'm at your service. Just tell me what to do."

"Well, you can start by popping the cork on that bottle of Merlot you have in your hand."

"That, I think I can handle."

Lisa was ready for that glass of wine. *I need to relax a little. I can't be this wound up the whole time. I'm liable to have a stroke.*

Katrina went to a drawer in the kitchen and pulled out a corkscrew. She handed it to Lisa, then went to the hutch to retrieve two wine glasses. She set them in front of Lisa. She involuntarily winked as she did it. She was hoping Lisa didn't notice but was sure she did.

They got to work making dinner, sipping their wine, and talking like they had known each other their whole lives. Katrina had Lisa cook the meat as she chopped vegetables. Before they knew it, they were done. They had 30 minutes to wait while the lasagna baked.

"You have a charming place," Lisa commented. "Can I get the grand tour?"

"Absolutely, that should kill enough time for the lasagna to get done."

She showed her through the living room, her home office, waved her past the bathroom, and they ended up in her bedroom.

"Wow, your house is amazing. This is possibly the biggest bedroom I've ever seen," Lisa said in awe.

"I've spent a lot of time decorating it. It's my first house. It's not much, but it's mine," she said.

"You've done well. Mmm, my stomach is growling. Is that wonderful-smelling lasagna done yet?"

Katrina smiled. "I hope so. I'm starving."

They made their way back to the kitchen. Lisa couldn't help but watch Katrina's white pants as they walked.

"Do you want another glass of wine?" Katrina asked as she turned to walk backward down the hall. She'd caught Lisa staring. "Were you looking at my ass?" she asked with mock shock.

"Absolutely not!" Lisa turned bright red.

"Too bad." Katrina smiled and turned back around. "So, that's a 'yes' to the wine?"

"Yep! I'll pour." Lisa got the wine and Katrina got the lasagna. They sat across from each other at her small table just off her kitchen.

"Wow, this is amazing lasagna! I think I might need a cigarette after this, it's so good," Lisa gushed.

"I think that's the best compliment I've ever gotten," Katrina said, blushing.

"If that's the best compliment you've ever gotten, you've been with the wrong people," she replied seriously.

"Oh, really? What haven't they told me?"

"That you're wonderful. You have the most amazing eyes. Eyes a person could get lost in. Perfect shoulders.

Flawless skin. The kind of personality that just makes me want to know everything there is to know about you," she said, looking into Katrina's eyes. *Damn wine. I would have never said that sober. How embarrassing.* "I'm sorry, I said too much. I'm sorry if I made you uncomfortable."

"You didn't make me uncomfortable at all. I have never felt as comfortable with someone as I do with you."

"So, can I ask you a stupid question?"

"You can ask me anything." She set down her fork, folded her hands under her chin, and gave Lisa her full attention.

"What were you expecting when you asked me over tonight?"

"Well, I wasn't really sure what to expect, to be honest. You intrigued me. I couldn't stop thinking about you," Katrina admitted, blushing again.

"Can I ask you another stupid question?"

"Of course." Katrina swallowed hard. For some reason she got those little butterflies again.

Lisa looked into those hypnotic eyes. *Just do it, before you lose your nerve.* "What would you do if I kissed you?"

"Why don't you try it and see?" Katrina sounded cool, even though she felt like she was going to lose it.

Lisa took a deep breath, stood up and walked around the table to Katrina. She took her hand and pulled her to her feet. She looked into Katrina's eyes, searching for any sign of resistance, but found none. She only saw a complete openness.

She brushed the hair back from that flawless cheek and wrapped her long fingers around the back of her neck. She felt like her heart was going to beat out of her chest. She pulled her close, feeling both of their pulses going crazy. Lisa bent her head to meet Katrina's lips, brushing them softly with her own.

Her lips were so soft, so inviting. She wanted to keep kissing them and never stop. She pulled back in spite of herself. Katrina looked up at her, eyes big with excitement. She still didn't look scared. Katrina licked her luscious lips.

Lisa couldn't resist any longer. She bent down again. This time her kiss was a little more firm, self-assured. Her lips tingled, her mind went blank. For that one moment, the only thing that existed was the two of them and that kiss.

Even though she didn't want to, Lisa pulled away. She had too. She had suddenly realized she had forgotten to breathe. Katrina's eyes were still closed, her lips still puckered; the memory of the kiss still visible on them.

Katrina opened her eyes and looked at Lisa like she was seeing her for the first time. She tried to speak but couldn't find the words. She knew she had fallen in love the moment their lips touched. She wanted to say those words so badly, but feared she would never see Lisa again.

"I... uh... wow. I think I need a cigarette now," Katrina said, smiling at Lisa.

"I could do that all night," Lisa whispered in Katrina's ear.

Lisa pulled Katrina against her body. She could feel her breathing, her pounding heart. She thought she should let her go, but her arms were not cooperating.

"Me too. I never knew a kiss could feel like that. I'm a little dizzy," Katrina admitted.

Lisa loosened her grip. "Maybe you should sit," she said, concerned.

"Please, don't let go," she said, her eyes pleading.

Lisa had no choice but to kiss her again. They kissed for what could've been forever, or just a moment, neither was sure. When they stopped to catch their breath again, Katrina looked up at Lisa.

"Stay the night," Katrina said. It wasn't a question.

"I would love nothing more, but I don't think that's a good idea. I don't want to ruin it. We have plenty of time for that."

Katrina bowed her head. She knew Lisa was right. "Come over tomorrow? We can go for a walk in the park."

"Absolutely, I'll be here early. I'll bring breakfast. I better go before it gets any harder to let go." She ran her hands down Katrina's arms and took her hands in hers. "Walk me out?"

"Of course."

They walked to the door holding hands, not really saying anything.

"I'll see you first thing in the morning, in just a few hours." Lisa smiled and kissed her again.

"Okay, I can't wait to see you again. Be careful driving home." Katrina smiled back. She opened the door unwillingly and watched Lisa walk down the driveway. She closed and locked the door as Lisa started her Jeep and drove off.

She got ready for bed, even though she was far from tired. She climbed into bed after she put on her favorite t-shirt and flipped on the TV. A few minutes later her phone was vibrating.

Just wanted to let u know I made it home. Cant wait 2 c u again

Thank u. I'll b counting the minutes till u cum back.

They texted back and forth until they fell asleep.

~4~

Lisa woke up early with a smile on her face. She wasn't sure if she had actually slept at all. She felt great, all the same. For the first time she could remember, she flew out of bed fully awake without her morning cup of coffee. She had met the love of her life; she didn't need coffee.

She quickly hopped in the shower. As she hurriedly scrubbed she decided she would run to her favorite bagel place. It would be quick, which meant she could see Katrina again that much sooner. She turned off the hot water after just a few minutes, but she felt clean.

She ran the towel over her naked, toned body. *Hmm, what to wear. Something comfy but not grungy. Jeans and a tank top will do. I look hot in a tank top.* She threw on some old jeans and a black tank top.

She almost ran to the bathroom to run a comb through her hair and brush her teeth. When she was done, she grabbed her keys and wallet and flew out the door. She made it to The Denver Bagel Company in record time. *What kind of bagel would Katrina eat? I think she would like...cinnamon raisin.*

"Give me two cinnamon raisin and two venti caramel macchiatos."

"Hey, no good morning? What the hell? I might spit in your coffee," the guy behind the counter joked. Lisa came here so often they knew her by sight.

"Sorry, I'm a little distracted this morning, Joe."

"That's alright, Lisa. Hmm, two bagels and two coffees? Who is she?" Joe smiled wryly.

"Someone very special. I can't wait to get back to her."

"I see. Well, I'll hurry then. I can't believe you left this special girl in your bed to come see me."

"I didn't. I had some extremely good self-control last night. I went home alone. But, I'm bringing her breakfast this morning. I left her place six hours ago, and I can't stand it," she gushed.

"Nice. Good for you! It's better if you wait. Even if it is just six hours. You know, bagels are an aphrodisiac, right? Bring these nice warm circles of love to her; she'll be putty in your hands," Joe said as he handed her the bag. "That's $12.58, sweetie."

She was getting impatient; this exchange was taking too long. As he handed back her card, Joe looked her in the eyes and said sincerely, "I've never seen you this happy before. You deserve it. Good luck."

"Thanks, Joe. But, I don't need luck, I have love." She smiled as she pushed through the door.

She raced to her Jeep. She couldn't wait another minute to see Katrina. *Thank God we don't live very far apart, only a few blocks to go. I sure hope she's awake.* She nearly broke the speed barrier those few blocks to her love's house.

When she got there, she practically floated to the door. She knocked and waited … and waited. She knocked again … still nothing.

Shit! She's still sleeping. Thinking quickly, she decided there had to be a hidden key somewhere. She set down their breakfast to search the porch. It only took her a few moments to find the fake rock that was hiding the key. *Damn it, Katrina. This is so unsafe. She's so naïve.*

She scooped up the bagels and coffee and let herself in. She walked down the hall to the bedroom. What she saw took her breath away.

Katrina was wearing an old gray t-shirt and white panties. *It must have been hot in here last night; she kicked all the blankets off.* Feeling a little dizzy, Lisa walked forward and set the food on the nightstand. She bent down and kissed that flawless forehead. Katrina's eyes fluttered open. Instead of screaming, which Lisa was terrified would happen, she smiled. "I was dreaming of you," she said sleepily.

"I thought I was dreaming," Lisa smiled back. "You looked perfect lying there."

Katrina blushed as she realized she wasn't covered by blankets. Sensing her embarrassment, Lisa pulled the blankets up over her smooth legs.

"I have coffee and bagels," Lisa said, nodding toward the nightstand.

"Mmmm, coffee. Why don't you get in with me? We can drink coffee and watch some TV?"

"Sounds perfect."

Lisa handed a coffee cup to Katrina. Then she kicked off her shoes and climbed in beside her. Katrina flipped channels until she found one of her favorite movies.

"Footloose?" Lisa asked.

"What do you have against Kevin Bacon?" Katrina was incredulous.

"Not a thing. I love this movie," Lisa grinned.

"Good, I might have had to kick you out of my bed if you didn't," Katrina said as she cuddled up to Lisa.

They snuggled most of the morning, watching the movie and talking intermittently. It was like they had done this every Sunday morning for years.

Katrina dozed off for a little while and left a small spot of spittle on Lisa's shirt. She woke up and wiped her mouth, embarrassed. She looked up at Lisa sheepishly.

"What did you do?" Lisa asked with a grin.

"Your shirt has a wet spot." She blushed. "I don't know how that happened."

"Sure, that's so gross!" She said, with mock disgust.

"I guess you need to take that shirt off then," Katrina smiled with mischief in her eyes..

"Nice try, Beautiful." Lisa couldn't help but smile at the feeble attempt to start something.

"Can't blame me for trying. How about that walk now? It looks like a gorgeous day out there."

"That sounds like a good plan. We can't waste the whole day in bed." She threw back the covers and stretched. She slipped her shoes on and peeked at Katrina on the opposite side of the bed.

She still hadn't put any pants on, and she looked very sexy. Almost too sexy to resist. *Damn my willpower!* She wanted so bad to make love to her at that very moment. But, she didn't want to do anything Katrina would regret. Katrina caught her staring and came around the bed to sit next to her.

"What's wrong sexy? You look like you're in pain," Katrina asked, stroking her hair.

"You have no idea how hard it is for me to resist you," Lisa admitted looking into her eyes.

"Then don't resist," she said simply.

"I'm scared. You're so perfect in every way. But, you're straight. What if you don't like it? What if I can't satisfy you?"

Katrina couldn't help but laugh. "I'm not straight, never have been. I put on a front to please my parents. I was so good I almost had myself convinced, until I met you anyway. I don't want to pretend anymore. Look at you, you're so self-assured and proud of who you are. I want to be like that. No more false, fake crap."

"So, you want to be with me so you can come out of the closet?" Lisa asked with pain on her face.

"No, meeting you made me *realize* that I want to be out of the closet." She looked like she was going to cry.

Lisa fell even harder for her at that moment. Katrina was so genuine, so true, and so perfect for her. She had to kiss her; there was no resisting now. She kissed her gently, burying her hands in her thick black hair. Katrina kissed her back, with her whole body. Lisa felt something wet touch her cheek. She pulled back to see tears streaming down Katrina's face. She was graceful even when she cried.

"What's wrong baby? Did I hurt you?" Lisa was scared; no one had ever cried when she kissed them before.

"I'm sorry. I don't know. I've never done that before. You're so amazing and gentle; I have never felt this way about anyone." She smiled apologetically through her tears.

Lisa wiped at her cheeks with shaking fingers. "I've never felt this way either," she said through shaking lips. "I think you need some fresh air. Come on Beautiful, it's time for our walk."

Katrina smiled feebly again and took Lisa's hand as they stood. The park was within walking distance, the weather was perfect, so they strolled lazily, holding hands.

"So, you never told me what you do for a living," Katrina said, suddenly realizing.

"I'm a vet. I run my own clinic. It's small right now, but business is growing."

"I should have guessed. You're so kind; it only makes sense that you would take care of animals. I find that incredibly endearing." *If I get any stronger feelings for her I may have a heart attack because my heart is too full of love,* Katrina thought.

"I guess." Now it was Lisa's turn to blush. "It's great doing what I love."

They walked and talked for a long time, not really paying attention to anything but each other.

"Oh my God!" Katrina exclaimed. "I totally forgot about my proposal! I have to write it by 8 a.m. tomorrow morning."

"Oh," Lisa said, disappointed. "I'll let you get to it then."

"No, please don't leave. I can put it off for a little longer. What time is it?" She looked at her watch. "Shit! It's already 5:30!"

Lisa stopped walking and pulled Katrina close. "How about we go back to your place. You can work on your proposal, and I'll make dinner while you work."

"That sounds wonderful," Katrina said, relieved. They walked quickly back to the house, hand-in-hand. Before they parted ways, Katrina stretched up on her toes to steal a kiss. "Thank you so much."

"I would do anything for you, darling. Now, go get to work." Lisa kissed her forehead and headed for the kitchen.

She searched the kitchen for ingredients to make something for dinner. *Wow, she doesn't have much. Well, I think I can find everything for spaghetti. It's not spectacular, but it'll be good.*

She hummed as she worked, just happy to be in the same house as Katrina. She wanted to go check on her, but didn't want to interrupt her work. So she stayed in the kitchen, happily making her spaghetti.

After she put the dinner on plates, she went to retrieve her love. She wandered down the hall, listening to the click of mad typing. She leaned on the doorframe and smiled, watching her work. Katrina felt her presence and looked up at her.

"Hey Beautiful, dinner's ready. You know, if I'm going to be making you dinner, you need to go to the grocery store," she teased.

"I'm sorry, I've been so busy. I usually just grab something on the way home. I don't like to cook for just me anyway. But, if you want to cook for me, I'll buy whatever you want." Katrina flashed her award-winning smile.

Lisa led the way to the kitchen. She was proud of her dinner.

"It smells wonderful," Katrina gushed. "I didn't realize how hungry I was. Please excuse me while I stuff my face." Katrina attacked the spaghetti as if she'd been starving for months.

"You're gorgeous, even with tomato sauce on your cheeks."

Katrina blushed, but couldn't say anything because her mouth was too full of noodles. They ate in relative silence, except for the noises of enjoyment coming from Katrina.

"That was the best spaghetti I have ever had. Oh my gosh, I am so full." She sat back and rubbed her satisfied belly.

"How's the proposal?" Lisa asked, smiling at Katrina's satisfaction.

"It's almost done. I can't believe I forgot about it. I guess someone distracted me all weekend."

"Well, get back to it. I'll clean up the kitchen," Lisa ordered.

"Yes, ma'am. Thank you so much for dinner. It was amazing." She hopped up from the table and brushed Lisa's cheek with a gentle kiss.

Lisa practically skipped around the kitchen as she cleaned. She hated cleaning, but for some reason, tonight she didn't mind. She finished wiping down the counters, and then went back down the hall. Katrina was still hard at work. She hated to leave, but Lisa knew she should. Katrina would never get it done with her there.

"Hey, darling, I'm going to head home. You look like you have a ton of work to do. Call me when you're finished, okay? No matter what time that is."

"Okay, let me walk you out, at least."

They walked to the door, Lisa behind with her arms around Katrina's shoulders. When they got to the door Katrina turned to face her. "Thank you for everything. Today was so great. I'll call you soon."

She pulled Lisa down to meet her mouth; they embraced for a long moment, exploring each other. Lisa's hands found the patch of skin on her clavicle, exposed from Katrina stretching up to meet her lips. It was so soft. As she ran her fingers across it, she felt Katrina shiver.

Finally, Lisa pulled back when she felt like she couldn't breathe. "Okay, Beautiful. I'm going. Get your report done. I'll be waiting for your call."

"Okay, I'll call you. Be careful going home. Text me when you get there. You know, so I don't worry."

"I will. We'll talk soon." She bent down to kiss those irresistible lips again. It was even harder to pull away this time, but somehow she managed. She begrudgingly let go and headed to her Jeep. It was almost physically painful for Lisa to leave. She didn't know how many more times she could actually leave to go back to her empty house.

~5~

The next day Katrina felt ready for her presentation at work. She ran through it again as she got dressed, although she kept getting distracted with thoughts of Lisa. *That can't happen during the presentation,* she told herself.

She decided she wouldn't talk to Lisa until afterward. That should help her keep her head in the game. This was a big deal; if she did well on this, she was up for a huge bonus.

As she drove to the office she afforded herself a daydream about Lisa. It was nothing specific, just how it felt when their lips met. She tingled every time she thought about it. As she pulled into her spot in the lot of her office building she told herself, *Okay, get your game face on. After you seal the merger, you can call her and celebrate.*

She set her stuff down at her desk and headed to the conference room. She prepared for her presentation, trying to clear her mind of anything not work-related. The board members filed into the room. *Game time,* she told herself. She pasted a confident smile on her face and greeted them all by name.

She nailed her presentation. Frank couldn't stop smiling, it was contagious. Katrina's face hurt from grinning, but she couldn't quit. After the last man in a suit filtered out, Frank jumped up from his seat at the end of the conference table. He grabbed Katrina and swung her around.

"You did it, kid! I knew there was a reason I keep you around," he shouted, planting a big wet kiss on her cheek.

"Oh my God! I can't believe it! Lunch is on me; we need to celebrate, Frankie!" she screeched as he continued to swing her. She was feeling a little dizzy but didn't care. This was the best feeling, except of course when Lisa's lips were pressed to hers.

"No way, I'm buying. I already have reservations at Henry's."

"That sounds great! I was so nervous this morning I didn't eat. Now I'm starving."

He finally set her down so he could look at his watch. "Perfect timing. The reservation is in 30 minutes."

"K, let me just go make a quick phone call and grab my bag," Katrina said as she almost ran out of the room. All she could think about at that moment was telling Lisa her good news. She grabbed the phone off the desk and dialed the already familiar number. It went to voicemail.

Damn, she must be busy. I'll just leave a quick message. After the beep, she said, "Hey, baby, just had some good news. Give me a call back when you can."

Shit, I called her baby. Is that okay? Will she be offended that I assume she's my baby? Oh well, too late now.

She grabbed her bag and headed out to meet Frank who was waiting in the hall. They rode in the same car to the restaurant. The senior partners were there waiting for them. Everyone kept telling Katrina what a great job she had done. She was getting so many pats on the back, she was almost sore.

Her mind was elsewhere, though. She kept checking her phone; nothing back from Lisa. She was starting to worry. *Maybe she had offended her?*

After lunch, it was back to the office to get started on all the work Katrina had outlined in her proposal. She was so busy she almost didn't have time to think about Lisa. Almost. She couldn't help but let little mini-day-dreams slip in every once in awhile. Before she knew it, it was five o'clock. She still hadn't heard from Lisa all day.

I knew it! She didn't like me calling her baby. I'm such a jerk. She drove home in silence, her big success all but forgotten.

She was so upset she didn't even notice the yellow Jeep sitting in front of her house until she was pulling into the driveway. When she finally did see it, she almost ran over her mailbox. She hit the brakes hard when she saw the cute blonde leaning against the Jeep. She slammed the car in park and jumped out. Before she could stop herself, she ran over and gave Lisa a huge hug.

"What're you doing here?" she blurted.

"I'm waiting on you," Lisa said smiling and looking oh-so-sexy. "I dropped my phone and cracked the screen this morning. When you called I didn't know it was you. I listened to your message but never got a chance to call you back. So, I decided to come get your good news first-hand."

"Oh! Yeah, my presentation went perfect. I sealed the merger!"

"Wow! That's amazing! I never had any doubt," Lisa said, as she scooped Katrina up and kissed her passionately.

When her feet were back on the ground, Katrina was a little red-faced. Partly because she was very excited to see Lisa and to know that she wasn't mad at her. And partly because Lisa had kissed her out in the front yard where anyone could see. She was a little worried about what her neighbors would think. She quickly pushed that thought out of her mind.

"Well, I think we need to celebrate. I decided that you should come over to my place for dinner. I don't cook during the week, but I know a great place for take-out not too far from here. What do you say?" Lisa asked, never taking her eyes off of Katrina's.

"You must have read my mind," Katrina replied with a smile. "Just let me change my clothes. I can't stand these pantyhose for another second!"

"Okay, even though I have to tell you, you look amazing in your power suit. But, I'll let you change. Do you mind if I come in with you?"

"I would mind if you didn't come. It's just sweats after a day like today, just as a warning."

Lisa couldn't help but smile. "You would look amazing in anything you wear." She grabbed Katrina's hand as they walked up to the house.

She was still mystified about how strongly she felt for Katrina. She knew logically that she shouldn't have feelings this quickly. But, she couldn't will herself to not feel this way.

She watched Katrina strip down to her bra and panties, which were a matching baby blue set. She had to sit on her hands to keep herself from jumping up off the bed and taking her.

She licked her lips as Katrina pulled a black tank top over her head, and swallowed hard watching her step into a pair of gray sweats. It hadn't been just words; she really did look hot no matter what she wore.

After Katrina slipped on a pair of black converse, she stepped out of the closet. Lisa looked up at her, speechless. She felt her cheeks get hot because she had gotten caught nearly drooling.

"Okay, I think I'm ready," Katrina said.

"Me, too." Lisa stood up on shaky legs.

"Are you okay? You look a little pale," Katrina asked her, concerned.

"I'm okay. Do you know how hard it was not to lay you down on the bed just now?"

"Not hard enough, I guess," she teased. "I was kind of hoping you would."

Lisa hugged her close. "In good time, Beautiful, in good time. I want it to be special for you."

"As long as it's with you, it will be special. I can be just as patient as you can."

They walked to the Jeep together. Lisa nodded back to the Volvo sitting in the driveway. "That's a nice ride. Are you sure you're okay with riding my Jeep? It's nothing special."

"Yep, I don't care what kind of car you drive, as long as I get to sit next to you." Katrina smiled and grabbed Lisa around the neck and kissed her deeply. Then she whirled around and hopped into the bucket seat.

They drove, just enjoying each other's presence. They pulled up to the restaurant, a place called Geo's. Katrina had never heard of it before.

Lisa leaned over and kissed her cheek. "I know it looks like a grease trap, but I promise they have the best guacamole you have ever tasted. I'll be right back."

Katrina sat in the Jeep waiting, daydreaming. She seemed to be doing a lot of that lately. It was really unlike her. She was what she considered a realist. She couldn't remember the last time she had actually daydreamed about anyone. Lisa just seemed to bring it out. She thought about what making love to her would be like.

She thought about Lisa's strong hands caressing every inch of her shaking body. She was startled out of her fantasy by the door opening on the driver's side. Katrina blushed, thinking that somehow her thoughts would show on her face.

Lisa was beaming. "Are you ready for the best Mexican food ever?"

"Absolutely! My stomach is growling now that I can smell it."

They were only a few blocks from Lisa's house.

"I have to tell you; my place is nothing like yours. It's small, but it's clean. And it's not mine; I rent. But, I've been there for three years. I never really needed much room for just me. They do let me have a pet though. His name is Jake."

"What kind of pet is it?" Katrina was curious. She had always wanted a pet, but never had the time to devote to one.

"He's a Siamese cat. I've had him for five years. A very good roommate. Well, here we are," she announced, pulling into the driveway to an old brown house. Lisa was right, it was small, but it looked comfortable.

As they walked in Katrina looked around. The front room was painted a deep blue, with art covering a majority of the walls. The kitchen was small, but clean. They sat down at the table, and Lisa happily unpacked the huge brown bag she had carried out of the restaurant.

"I'm so excited for you to try these tacos. Better than you'll find in Mexico," Lisa said excitedly.

"It smells great. You get to watch me stuff my face again. I swear I don't usually scarf my food," Katrina said with an apologetic smile.

"It's okay. I like to watch you eat. I can see the pleasure all over your face. Now, tell me what you think."

Lisa pushed a Styrofoam box toward Katrina. It was filled with three huge tacos, beans, and Spanish rice.

Katrina picked up a massive taco and wrapped her mouth around it. She couldn't help herself, she moaned with pleasure. Lisa was right, it was the best taco she had ever had. She opened her eyes to Lisa smiling, watching her.

Katrina realized how much noise she had been making at that moment and stopped chewing altogether. "Sorry," she mumbled around her mouthful of food.

"Don't apologize." Lisa took her hand. "I think it's sexy."

"It's gross," Katrina countered.

"Not at all," Lisa kissed her hand, and then let it go so she could grab one of her tacos.

They ate quickly, only stopping long enough to take large gulps of water.

"Oh my God! I think I might explode," Katrina said as she sat back in her chair and patted her belly.

"Me, too. Maybe we should take a walk. That will help us not vomit," Lisa suggested.

Katrina stood up and reached for Lisa's hand. Together they walked to the front door and down the front steps.

"Where do we go from here?" Katrina said, looking into Lisa's eyes.

"This way," Lisa said as she gently pulled Katrina alongside her.

They walked slowly around the block, lazily swinging their hands between them. Lisa pointed out the little landmarks around her neighborhood; the community flower garden, the kids' basketball court, the tree she backed into and left a small smudge of yellow paint on.

"It's home. We're like a family around here. Everyone looks out for everyone," Lisa said, concluding the tour as they climbed the steps in front of her little house.

"It's a great neighborhood. You can feel the love walking down the street. I bet you're going to miss it."

"Why would I miss it?" Lisa asked with a puzzled look.

"When you move into my house, of course," she said, smiling.

"Ah, I see. Don't you think that's a little presumptuous? We haven't even slept together yet," Lisa said, kissing her forehead lovingly.

"Well, it's not for lack of trying," Katrina pouted.

Lisa took both of her hands in hers and looked into her deep blue eyes. "I promise you, when the time is right, we will. And it'll be the most amazing moment of our lives."

"I'm going to hold you to that," Katrina promised.

"You can hold me to whatever you want," Lisa said, as she pulled her close and rested her chin on the top of her head. "I better get you home, Beautiful. It's late."

Katrina pulled her head back, "Are trying to get rid of me?" she teased.

"Not at all; I would keep you forever if I could. But, you look exhausted."

"I'm not tired," she replied, stifling a yawn. "Alright, maybe a little."

"Let's get you home. I'll tuck you in, okay?"

"Okay, you tucking me in sounds good. You could hold me until I fall asleep if you want to."

"Hmm... I might just do that. I love holding you."

She pulled herself away so she could lead Katrina back down the front steps to the Jeep. They made the short drive back to Katrina's house in silence, just holding hands and enjoying each other's presence.

Once back in the house, Katrina headed to the bathroom to wash her face and brush her teeth.

Lisa went to the bed and kicked off her shoes, then sat up on top of the blankets. Katrina came out of the bathroom minus her sweats.

Lisa forgot how to breathe for a moment. It was getting harder and harder to resist this incredibly sexy woman. Lisa had never seen someone look so sexy in a tank top and panties. She couldn't remember any other woman at all. The only woman in the whole world was standing right in front of her.

"You have to stop doing that," Lisa said.

"Doing what?" Katrina asked coyly as she slipped into the bed.

"Looking irresistible."

"I think you're crazy. I just have this old tank top on."

"Yeah, I know."

Lisa was trying to relax but it wasn't working. She put her hand under Katrina's chin and pulled her close to kiss her softly. Then not so softly. Her hands tangled in her hair; ran down her neck, her lips followed them. Her hand caressed one full breast, then the other. She knew she should stop, had to stop, but she couldn't. She had been holding back for so long; she felt she might explode if she did stop. Her lips found their way back up to Katrina's. She kissed her passionately until she was dizzy. She pulled back, looking into Katrina's love-filled eyes.

"Please don't stop," Katrina whispered.

"I have to. I really don't want to. You're irresistible, Sexy. But, not now. Not like this. I want it to be special. Soon, I promise. Now, lay down so you can get some sleep. I'll hold you till you're snoring."

"Okay, but you shouldn't kiss me like that unless you're going to finish. I love that you want to make it special, so I guess I'll forgive you this time," Katrina said as she cuddled up under Lisa's arm.

A few minutes later Katrina's breathing slowed and her body relaxed against Lisa. She could stay here all night listening to her breathe, but she needed to get home. She stealthily slipped out of bed, put her shoes on and tiptoed out of the house.

She drove home not really paying attention to the road. She was thinking about that kiss, about how easy it would have been to make love to her.

She was kicking herself for not taking the opportunity. Now she had to think of something really special to do for the first time they actually did make love.

~6~

The rest of the week was busy for the both of them. Lisa had emergencies nearly every day at the clinic; she was staying until nine every night. Katrina had huge computer issues that kept her in the office even later than that.

They had not seen each other since that Monday when Lisa held Katrina, falling in love deeper with every passing second. They still found time to talk every day, even if it was only a few minutes at a time.

Now it was Friday, and things seemed to be working out for them both. Lisa closed the clinic at three that afternoon because she had purposefully not scheduled any afternoon appointments. She had been thinking about what to do for Katrina all week. She was dying, not seeing Katrina for a whole four days.

Lisa had made reservations at the nicest restaurant in town, The Matchbook. People would usually go there to propose, but nothing like that would happen tonight. It was too soon for that. Lisa could see that happening for them sometime, this night was about celebrating just being together.

This was the first time they were having an official date.

On her way home Lisa stopped by the flower shop. She picked out the most exquisite half dozen roses they had, light pink, like the color of Katrina's lips.

She went home for a shower and to slip into her new clothes she'd bought just for tonight. She detested shopping, but she felt like she had to look her best to take out the most gorgeous woman on the planet.

She took her time in the shower, washing every part of her body twice. She shaved her legs and her armpits.

She even washed her hair twice, and used a little conditioner.

When she got out, she brushed her teeth and cut her nails. She painstakingly fixed her hair, putting every strand into place.

When everything was perfect, she went to her closet and pulled out her new clothes; a pair of khaki pants and a soft light blue polo. She thought it made her eyes stand out. She'd even bought new shoes for the occasion; dark brown loafers. She scrutinized herself in the full-length mirror on the back of her bedroom door.

She stared for a long time. *Are you good enough to be with Katrina? She deserves the best. Maybe bring her a present to go along with the flowers. You still have time before you pick her up.* She grabbed her wallet and the flowers and headed to the Jeep.

She went to Shamus Jewelers. She looked through all the glass cases; nothing seeming to be right for Katrina. All the jewels paled in comparison to the beauty Katrina held.

Finally, she came across a ruby solitaire necklace. It was perfect. It was expensive, but Lisa didn't care. She watched the salesman place the necklace into a black box.

She couldn't stop smiling as she paid and headed back to the Jeep. She looked at the clock in the dash; she was going to be right on time. Everything seemed to be working out just right.

Lisa pulled up to Katrina's house; her heart was pounding so fast she could hear it. She sat taking deep breaths. *You better hurry up. She's probably wondering what you're doing.*

So, she took one last deep breath and grabbed the flowers and little black box off the seat next to her. Lisa concentrated on every step she took to the front door, afraid of tripping over her own feet in her excitement. She rang the doorbell, and her heart leaped into her throat.

She listened to the soft footsteps padding toward the door, her heart beating harder with every step. She listened to the lock turn, holding her breath, and watched the door slowly swing open, feeling lightheaded.

Katrina was a vision in her black low-cut dress, her hair pinned up, with a few strands of dark hair framing her face. Lisa let out the breath she had been holding.

"Wow, you look amazing. I didn't think it was possible for you to look any better than you usually do," she said as she stood there on the porch, trying to keep herself from falling down because her knees were weak.

"You look very hot yourself," Katrina flushed. "Are you going to come in? I'm almost ready."

Lisa walked past her into the house. Katrina smelled amazing, even more so than usual.

"So, since this is our first official date, I brought you flowers," Lisa said, handing Katrina the roses.

Katrina took them and gently smelled them. "They're lovely. Thank you. I have the perfect vase for them." She carried them into the kitchen to retrieve it front the cabinet under the sink. She filled it with water and carefully placed them in the vase, arranging them so she could see every flower. She turned to face Lisa, beaming.

"I almost forgot to kiss you," she said as she reached up for Lisa's cheek. She pulled her face down to meet hers and kissed her lips gently.

"You're shaking, are you okay?" Katrina whispered, looking into her eyes.

Lisa swallowed hard. "I'm perfect. I just can't get over how exquisite you look tonight. I have something else for you too."

"You're going to spoil me," Katrina said, stroking her cheek.

"Close your eyes."

Lisa took the black box out, and with shaking hands, opened it and lifted the necklace out. She fumbled with the clasp, went behind Katrina and slid the ruby across her ivory skin, fastening it behind her.

"Okay, you can open your eyes now."

Katrina brought her hand up to her neck to feel what the weight was. Her eyes lit up and she ran to the bathroom to inspect it closely. Lisa was a little worried, so she followed the scent of Katrina's perfume down the hall. She found Katrina standing in front of the mirror, tears in her eyes. She rushed to her.

"What's wrong? What did I do? I'm sorry," she said, panicking.

Katrina turned to face her. "It's stunning," she said in a tear-choked voice. "I can't believe you did this. It's the most beautiful thing I have ever received."

"It's not nearly as stunning as you. Now, don't ever scare me like that again," she replied, wiping Katrina's cheeks. "We're going to be late. Get your shoes. There are more surprises in store for you."

"I don't know if I can handle any more surprises. I can't wait to see where we're going. I'm starving, like always." She went to her closet and pulled out her black stilettos. With them, she was almost as tall as Lisa. She grabbed her handbag off the dresser and headed to meet Lisa in the front room. "I'm ready."

So am I, Lisa thought. "Alright, let's do it, Beautiful."

They drove to the restaurant, Katrina trying to guess where they were going to whole time. She never did guess, until Lisa put on her turn signal to go into the parking lot. "You are not taking me here!" she shrieked. "How did you get reservations?"

"Don't worry about it. I pulled some favors." Lisa smiled and kissed the back of her hand.

"You're spending way too much money on me."

"Maybe we shouldn't see each other anymore; I'm going to go bankrupt," Lisa teased. "Seriously, you're worth every penny. Don't worry about the money. I own my own business, remember?"

"I remember. I'm not worth it."

"Not another word," Lisa interrupted. "You're worth it. Now, let me spoil you." She hopped out of the Jeep and ran around to Katrina's side to open the door for her. She held out her hand and helped her out. They walked into the restaurant holding hands.

"How can I help you?" the Maître D' asked as they walked in.

"We have a reservation for Thomas," Lisa said.

"Ah, right this way ladies." He walked them to a quiet table in the back of the dining room. "I hope you enjoy our finest table, ladies," he said, pulling out Katrina's chair for her.

"Thank you very much," Lisa replied.

After he had left, Katrina grabbed Lisa's hands, "The best table? Who do you know?"

"The owner has a very old dog, which I've taken care of my whole career. The last time I saved Bubba from certain death Mr. Lambarto promised me I could have this table whenever I wanted. I hadn't taken him up on it until tonight. I was waiting for a special person to share it with."

"Wow, you must be a really great vet."

"Just one of my many talents," Lisa laughed.

"I have no doubt," Katrina said and squeezed Lisa's hands.

"Well, I hope you don't mind, but I already ordered. So, we don't have to mess with the menus. We can spend all our time concentrating on each other."

"Wow, you're so thoughtful. I don't know if I can get used to this."

"You better. Because this is how I intend to treat you. You deserve to be treated like a princess."

Before Katrina could object, the first course arrived. It was a medley of mushrooms. Lisa picked one up with her fork and fed it to Katrina. She watched as she completely enjoyed it, finding the pleasure on her face very erotic.

She stabbed another mushroom and stuck it in her own mouth. They ate the rest of the appetizer this way, enjoying watching each other eat. Next, the waiter brought out the bottle of wine Lisa had ordered, a nice merlot.

After he filled both of their glasses, Lisa raised hers to Katrina. "To many more nights just like this."

Katrina touched her glass to Lisa's. "Here, here."

The conversation flowed during the rest of their meal. They were meant for each other. It was like they had already been together forever. Maybe in some way they had.

They ate dessert the same way they ate their appetizer, Lisa feeding them both. They sat for a while just talking and finishing their bottle of wine.

When they had finally finished it off, Lisa took Katrina's hands in hers. "Are you ready for your next surprise?"

"Sure, as long as it means this night doesn't have to end," she replied.

Lisa stood and went around the table to help her to her feet. She wrapped her arm around Katrina's shoulders and guided her to the door.

They drove to a deserted parking lot not far from Lisa's house. She put the Jeep in park and turned to face Katrina.

"I'm not a very good dancer, but I would like to dance with you."

"Here? How are we going to do that?"

"I made a special playlist for just for this occasion." The first song started. It was Depeche Mode. Lisa got out and walked around the Jeep to the passenger side. She opened the door and held out her hand. "May I have this dance?"

Katrina took her hand. "I can't think of anyone I would rather dance with."

They danced close as the music streamed from the Jeep's speakers. They danced through a few songs. They probably could've danced all night, but Lisa had other plans.

She pulled back so she could look into Katrina's face. "Thank you, that was the best dance I have ever had. Now it's time for the next surprise. Can you handle it?" she asked with a smile.

"I don't know, I think I might be surprised out," Katrina teased.

"I think you can handle it. It's the best one of the night."

"Okay, I'll suck it up and take one more." Katrina smiled and kissed Lisa's soft lips.

They got back in the Jeep and headed to Lisa's house. She had purposely chosen that parking lot so it would only take a couple minutes to get home. They walked into the dark house, hand-in-hand.

"You have to close your eyes one more time. I promise it will be worth it."

Katrina obliged willingly. She could hear Lisa moving around, but couldn't figure out what she was doing.

She heard soft music start to play, smelled what she thought was lavender, she felt Lisa return to her side.

"Okay, keep them closed. I'm going to lead you to the final—and best—one." She took Katrina's hand and led her down the short hallway to the bedroom. "Okay, now you can open."

Katrina opened her eyes to see the bedroom lit by candles; she saw the incense burning; saw the look in Lisa's eyes, so intense but so loving at the same time. She was speechless.

"I told you I wanted it to be special," Lisa said as she caressed her cheek. Her hand wrapped around the back of her neck, and pulled Katrina gently to her. She kissed her lips softly, savoring the way Katrina tasted.

She let her hands roam all over her body. She ran them across her shoulders, down her back; her hands found the zipper to her dress. She slowly pulled the zipper down, exposing her lower back. Her hands back up to her shoulders to slide her dress straps down, exposing her perfect breasts. She pushed it down past her waist; she was now completely naked except for her shoes.

Lisa pulled her mouth away from Katrina's and trailed it down her soft neck. She made it to one supple breast, then the other. She felt Katrina's body respond to the gentle touch of her lips brushing her erect nipples. Her mouth somehow found its way back up to Katrina's.

She wasn't holding back now. She kissed her firmly, passionately. She guided her to the bed, laying her down.

She smiled when she saw the shoes still on her feet. She bent down and slipped them off gently. She stood for a moment, just admiring the beauty on the bed. Now the only thing she was wearing was the ruby necklace.

"Is everything okay?" Katrina breathed.

Lisa smiled. "Everything is perfect."

She pulled off her own shirt and shoes, then her pants and lowered herself on top of Katrina. Katrina's hands traced her back, feeling every contour. She felt her way down Lisa's arms, then up to her hair. Her fingers ran through the blonde locks, grabbing gently as she became more excited by the passionate kisses Lisa was giving her. She had no idea what to expect, but she was tingling with anticipation.

Lisa could hardly contain herself. Her hands trailed along Katrina's sides. She moved her mouth down again to her neck, kissing her earlobes.

She stopped long enough to look at Katrina's face; she had to make sure she was enjoying this as much as she was. Katrina was biting her lip; Lisa took that as a good sign. She continued on, caressing her collarbones with her lips. She moved down to her perfect breasts again, her mouth exploring every inch. She moved down to her navel, tracing it with her tongue. She smiled as Katrina let out a little gasp. Still kissing her belly, she let her hands travel down to her thighs. The skin there was smooth and warm. She could wait no longer.

She took her mouth down to the sublime, warm, wet place between her legs. It was as flawless as the rest of her. Just a small patch of hair above the plump lips. She spread them with trembling fingers; she could feel the waves of excitement rolling off of Katrina's body.

She kissed the soft point of her clitoris, felt her body come up to meet her mouth. She buried her face in the warmth. She tasted amazing. She listened to her moaning, growing louder every second.

Katrina's hands rubbed Lisa's arms. Lisa could feel her pleasure mounting with each stroke of her tongue. She knew what was coming, knew she should try to make it last longer, but she was so excited herself she couldn't slow down.

She was almost frantic when she felt Katrina's body tighten under her firm grasp. She pushed on to guide her over the edge. Katrina's legs began to shake, and then she let out a sound of pure ecstasy. Lisa could feel the waves of pleasure as they pulsed out of Katrina's body. She held her and pressed on firmly to complete her orgasm. She only stopped when Katrina's body relaxed against the bed. Her breath was jagged and fast.

Lisa brought herself up to lay next to her. Katrina turned her head toward her, her eyes heavy, and kissed Lisa deeply. She wrapped her arms around her. Katrina's arms own were still shaking; her whole body was for that matter.

Lisa held her until her breathing was almost back to normal. "Well, was that worth the wait?" she asked, kissing her forehead.

"It was by far the best surprise of the night. I hope you don't expect me to leave. I don't think I can stand."

"Nope, you're staying right here where I can hold you all night while you sleep. You're so peaceful and pretty when you sleep."

"Good, because I may just pass out right now. You're amazing. I never thought it could be like that."

"Shh, just sleep. We have the rest of our lives for you to tell me what an amazing lover I am."

"Okay, Love. Just hold me." She kissed Lisa's lips sleepily and rested her head on her chest.

Lisa laid there for a long time, just listening to Katrina's breathing. With every breath, she became more sure that this was the last woman she would ever hold like this.

~7~

The next morning Katrina woke up first; Lisa was still holding her. She had never had been able to sleep like that before; she always had to have her own space. But, it felt so natural to wake up in Lisa's arms. She nestled closer. Lisa stirred and held her just a little tighter. Katrina laid there enjoying the sensation of Lisa's warmth against her back. She thought about the night before.

She had never known such pleasure. Now she knew what she had been missing all those years by denying who she was. She knew now, in this instant, that Lisa was her soulmate. She rolled carefully to face her. She could be completely happy waking up next to her every morning for the rest of her life.

She laid there watching Lisa sleep until she started thinking about coffee. She thought it would be romantic to have coffee ready when Lisa woke up. She slipped carefully out of the bed, making her way to the kitchen. She searched the cabinets until she found the coffee. She sat at the table until it was done, made two cups and headed back to the bedroom.

Lisa watched Katrina walk down the hall, naked, carrying two cups of coffee. Lisa couldn't help but smile; it was the most perfect sight she had ever seen.

"Well, I think this is the best wakeup call I have ever had," she said as Katrina handed her a steaming cup.

Katrina blushed a little. "I thought you would still be asleep."

"I'm glad I wasn't," Lisa said, sipping her coffee. "How are you feeling this morning?"

"Like I had the best sex of my life last night," Katrina answered.

"Oh, really?" Lisa grinned. "Nice to know the bar is set so low."

"Hardly. You were amazing. I have never passed out like that after sex. You should take that as a compliment."

"I do. Do you want to do it again?"

"My legs are still shaking from the last time. I don't know if I can get used to that," Katrina replied.

Lisa set her coffee cup down and looked at Katrina. "Can I tell you something?" she asked with a serious look on her face.

"You can tell me anything."

"I don't want to scare you. But, this has been the best week of my life. I have never felt like this about anyone. You're so amazing in every way. I don't remember what life was like without you, and I don't want to. Katrina, I love you." She said it all in one breath.

Katrina sat dazed, looking into her eyes. She didn't know what to say, so she kissed her. She couldn't stop. She knew she felt exactly the same way, but was scared to say it out loud.

Before she knew it, she was lying on her back, and Lisa was coaxing another orgasm from her. When her body had stopped pulsing from the pleasure, and her breathing had almost returned to normal, she found her voice.

"I love you, too," Katrina said, looking deeply into Lisa's eyes. "I knew it from the moment I hugged you in the parking lot after lunch that first day. You're the most amazing person I have ever met. You have the biggest heart, the kindest eyes, and the gentlest hands. You're everything I have ever wanted, but I didn't think anyone like you actually existed."

Now it was Lisa's turn to be speechless. She had found the woman of her dreams, and that woman felt the same way about her. She couldn't believe it. She felt like she might throw up.

"Really? How can you be so sure?" she asked as she swallowed hard, willing her coffee to stay put.

"I can't explain it, I just know," Katrina said simply.

Lisa took Katrina's face in her hands, looked into her eyes for a long moment and then kissed her softly. It was a gentle loving kiss, the kind of kiss that says things that words cannot.

They stayed in bed kissing and holding each other until neither of them could ignore the growling in their stomachs.

"Let's get dressed and head to the kitchen, Beautiful. I make some mean scrambled eggs." Lisa stood and headed to the dresser to pull a white t-shirt and a pair of old black sweats out.

Katrina smiled as she watched her dress. "Umm, I didn't really think I was staying the night, so I didn't bring any extra clothes."

"I guess you're just going to have to go naked," Lisa teased as she pulled out a large t-shirt and threw it to Katrina.

Lisa stood watching as Katrina slowly got to her feet and pulled the black cotton shirt over her head. "Hmm, you look good in my clothes."

"I know." Katrina smiled as she walked across the room to kiss those lips she just couldn't get enough of.

"You better cut that out if we're ever going to make it to the kitchen," Lisa said when she was finally able to pull herself away.

"Fine, I'll let you feed me," Katrina mock-pouted and took Lisa's hand as they walked to the kitchen.

Katrina watched Lisa scramble eggs, in awe. *Is there anything this woman can't do?* Katrina asked herself.

"Here are the best scrambled eggs you'll ever taste in your life, Beautiful."

"They look amazing," she said as she dug in. "Oh my God, they *are* the best scrambled eggs I've ever tasted," she said around a huge mouthful of eggs.

Lisa smiled at the cuteness of her talking with her mouth full. *What a dork I am,* she thought. *I just think everything about her is cute. I have officially lost it.*

"Why are you staring at me?" Katrina asked, studying Lisa's face.

"Sorry, you just look so cute when you stuff your face," Lisa replied.

Katrina blushed. "I can't help it. I must have burned a lot of calories last night ... and this morning."

"Don't apologize," Lisa said as she filled her own mouth with eggs. They ate in silence, just enjoying the food, and being together.

They spent the whole day together, not really doing much, just being with each other. That night, they curled up on the couch at Lisa's house to watch movies. Katrina fell asleep in Lisa's lap. When the movie was over, Lisa scooped her up and carried her to the bedroom. Katrina didn't wake up until she laid her on the bed.

"I love you," she mumbled as her eyes opened half way. Lisa bent and kissed her forehead before walking around the bed and climbing in next to her. Katrina instinctively rolled over and cuddled up next to Lisa.

That was the same position they were in when Lisa awoke in the morning. It was her turn to slip out of bed and make coffee while her love slept. She wasn't naked, but she still looked like heaven as Katrina watched her walk down the hall with a steaming cup in each hand.

They spent every morning like this for the next week. They alternated between each other's houses, not being able to spend an entire day away from one another.

The following Monday, Katrina was in her office, working hard as usual. Her boss came to the door.

"You have had that shit eating grin on your face for weeks. What's going on with you?" Frank asked.

Katrina blushed, she didn't realize she had been smiling non-stop since she fell in love with Lisa. She decided she had to tell someone; she had not been brave enough to tell her parents yet.

"I met someone," she said quietly.

"Well, who's the lucky son of a bitch?"

Katrina took a deep breath. "Her name is Lisa." She waited for the news to sink into Frank's brain.

"Well, I'm happy for you kiddo. I have never seen you so happy before. You know I need to meet her to give her the ol' 'Frank seal of approval.'"

Katrina was shocked by his response. She jumped up, ran around her desk, and threw her arms around the heavy-set man. "Thank you!" was all she could say.

"Maybe you can bring her to the house Saturday. I'll have Marla whip up her famous beef stroganoff."

"That sounds wonderful, we'll be there."

"Alright, be there at eight."

Katrina smiled as he walked out of the room. Frank had been the closest thing to family that she had since moving to Denver. His approval was important to her. *Maybe my parents won't take it as hard as I think they will. I need to just bite the bullet and tell them,* she thought to herself, as she hummed and smiled. She was so happy that the joy had to make its way out of her body somehow.

That night over dinner, Katrina told Lisa about her conversation with Frank. Lisa was excited to be able to meet Frank, she had heard so much about him. The lovebirds had been so engrossed with each other, they had not been around other people since starting their romance.

"I guess it's time we go public, huh?" Lisa said with a wink.

"I'll have to share your attention sometime. I have been selfish with you," Katrina replied.

When Saturday came, the couple grabbed a few bottles of their favorite wines and headed to Frank's large house across town.

Katrina looked as stunning as ever in a green silk tea dress, black peep-toe heels, and of course, her ruby necklace. The green of the dress set off her eyes, which shimmered with every smile.

As they reached the door, Katrina closed her eyes to calm herself. It was very important to her for Frank to like Lisa. Although, she wasn't sure how anyone couldn't see how amazing Lisa was. Katrina looked at her as she rang the bell.

Lisa, looked dapper in her lavender dress shirt and khaki pants. Lisa smiled nervously at her love, Katrina instinctively smiled back and grabbed a quick kiss before the door opened.

"Well, hey there!" a jolly Frank greeted them. "Early, as usual, my dear." He wrapped his arm around Katrina and kissed her on the cheek.

"Frank, this is Lisa. Lisa, Frank."

Lisa stuck out her hand, which Frank grabbed to pull her in for a hug. "Handshakes are for the boardroom."

"I guess I should have warned you, Frank is a hugger," Katrina blushed.

Without skipping a beat, Lisa wrapped her arms around the smiling man.

"Glad to meet you, Frank."

Katrina was impressed that nothing seemed to phase Lisa.

Just then, a pretty woman with black hair, just speckled with a few white strands, walked into the entryway to see what was going on.

"For heaven's sake, Frank, let the poor girls in already!" She walked over to Katrina and hugged her tightly. "I have missed you lately, my dear."

"I have missed you too, Marla. I haven't seen much of anybody lately, besides Lisa and Frank."

"I have scarcely seen Frank myself, with all the extra hours the two of you have been putting in. This must be Lisa," she said, shifting her gaze to the slender woman her husband was finally letting out of his strong grip.

This time Lisa was ready. She gently wrapped her right arm around Marla and kissed her cheek. "Thank you for having me in your home. Something smells incredible."

"The pleasure is all mine, darling. I hope you have an appetite as healthy as Katrina, I made enough to feed a small army."

Lisa smiled. "I don't think anyone can match Katrina's appetite, but I'll do my best. I hope you like Cabernet." She held up the brown bag from the liquor store.

"Well, we must see what you brought." Marla grabbed Lisa's hand, and off they went to the kitchen to find the wine opener and four glasses.

The kitchen was bigger than any Lisa had ever been in. It was white with all stainless steel appliances; every gadget she could think of was lined up along the counter. The smell coming from the stove was intoxicating. Lisa's belly grumbled.

"Will you do the honors?" Marla asked, handing the opener to Lisa.

"It would be my pleasure," Lisa grinned. She couldn't believe how comfortable she felt with this woman she had just met. She was so kind and welcoming, like a mother. Something Lisa knew little about; her own mother had left when she was little. She was left to be raised by her gruff father, along with her four brothers.

"Cheers!" Marla said, clinking glasses with Lisa. They sipped the luscious wine and savored the multilayered flavor before Marla nodded approval.

"Great pick, Lisa! I love a woman that knows her wine!"

The foursome ate dinner, talking like they were old friends. Lisa enjoyed herself a thousand times more than she had expected. When it was time to leave, she was almost sad to go.

"Thank you for a lovely evening," Lisa said at the door. "I don't think I'll need to eat for a week!"

They drove home in silence; not an uncomfortable silence, a happy silence, full of contentment.

Katrina grabbed Lisa's hand as she drove, smiling. As they pulled into the driveway of Katrina's house, she looked over at Lisa. "Would you please spend the night with me?"

"Like you even have to ask!" Lisa grinned. She had an overnight bag stuffed in the back seat for just such an occasion. She grabbed her bag and they headed inside.

They were both so tired, they just fell into bed. They snuggled up together and fell right asleep.

~8~

They didn't wake until they heard the doorbell ring the next morning. Katrina leaped out of bed to see who could be there so early on a Sunday morning. She looked through the peephole and gasped.

By this time Lisa was by her side, "Who is it, my love?"

"It's my parents!" she exclaimed, near terror.

"Should I sneak out the back?" Lisa asked, reading into the look of terror on her face.

"No, I want you to meet them. Bite the bullet," Katrina said, pulling the door open. "Mom! Dad! I'm so surprised to see you!"

"We haven't heard from you. We were worried," Katrina's mom accused. She was a large woman; dressed in an ankle-length black dress, a black hat, and what Lisa could only describe as Amish shoes. She spotted Lisa, peeking around Katrina's shoulder.

"Did you get a roommate, dear?" asked this house of a woman.

Katrina turned bright red. "No, Momma. This is my … my girlfriend," she stuttered.

The large woman and the stick of a man behind her looked shocked. Katrina's mother quickly regained her composer. "Well, aren't you going to introduce us, Kitty?"

Katrina hated when her mother called her that. She felt like a child. "Of course, Mother. This is Lisa. Lisa, these are my parents, Mildred and Virgil."

Lisa stuck out her hand. "Nice to meet you," she said, plastering the biggest smile she could muster on her still-sleepy face.

Katrina's mother answered with a tight-lipped smile, "How do you do?" she seethed, taking Lisa's hand in a limp grasp.

The thin man standing at the back of the porch finally found his voice, "I'm starving! How about we all go get some breakfast?" He knew Katrina wouldn't pass up breakfast.

"That is a great idea, Daddy!" Katrina pushed past the woman, who looked as is she had eaten a bowl of lemons, to squeeze the frail man tightly. "We'll be ready in five minutes! Please, come in and get comfortable."

She gestured to the old, but comfortable-looking couch. Mildred stepped carefully over the threshold, not taking her eyes off of Lisa.

The young lovers made their way to the bedroom for a quick change. Lisa could feel the distain in Katrina's mother's glare. *Has she not told her parents about me?*

Lisa felt quite uneasy about the whole situation as she pulled her Nirvana t-shirt over her head.

"Do you want me to go, so you can have breakfast with your parents? I know it's been awhile since you've seen them," she offered, forcing a smile. She hoped Katrina wouldn't see the nervous energy behind it.

"Don't be silly," Katrina replied. "They have to get to know you sometime." Katrina's smile was a bit shaky.

"Did you tell them about me?" Lisa had to know what she was walking into.

"Honestly, no. I haven't spoken to them much in the last few months. I have been busy with work and now you."

"So, they don't know you're gay?" Lisa was bewildered. She had never been in a situation like this before.

"No, I told you, they're very old-fashioned. That's one of the reasons I have always dated men. That's what they expected."

AMANDA WRAY

"So, now what are you going to do?"

Katrina was a bit off put by the tone of Lisa's inquisition. "I am a big girl. It's time I stopped being afraid of my mother."

By this time both women were dressed. Katrina turned to go out the bedroom door, but Lisa stopped her first.

"I love you." Lisa said, looking deep into those deep brown eyes. "I am proud of you for being so brave."

Brave! Katrina thought. *I might just shit myself at the breakfast table!*

"I love you too," she replied out loud, kissing her love's lips gently. They walked into the living room again, ready to go.

"Do you want to ride with us? There is plenty of room in Lisa's Keep," Katrina asked her silent parents sitting stiffly on the couch.

"Jeep! Heavens no! I do not want to mess up my hair," her mother replied in a tone that said 'how dare you!' "We'll take Daddy's car."

"Yes, ma'am," Katrina said, bowing her head dutifully.

The ride to the restaurant was painfully silent. Katrina clutched Lisa's hand with all her strength. Lisa thought she might lose a finger if they didn't go to a place close by. Luckily, Katrina's father found a Denny's a couple of miles from the house. They climbed out of the car, but not before Lisa gave Katrina's steely hand one last squeeze of motivation.

They all sat down and silently looked over the menu. After they had all ordered, Katrina took a deep breath. *Oh, shit! Here it comes!* Lisa couldn't help but think.

"Mom, dad," Katrina began, "there is something I need to tell you. Something that I have been keeping

65

from you for a long time." Now Katrina was the one fighting the urge to get sick.

"Oh, dear. Some things are meant to be kept a secret," her mother replied. "Good secrets keep good families."

"No," Katrina said, not losing her resolve, "secrets don't keep good families. They hurt people. I'm tired of living a lie. I'm gay. And I'm in love."

"Oh! That is just nonsense! People aren't born gay! It's something the TV puts in their heads. We'll get you some help, dear. It will be okay." Her mother stared unblinking into her daughter's eyes.

"Oh, stop, Mildred." This was the first time her father had spoken since she opened the door. "Kat is happy, you can see that. Let her be happy."

Katrina shot a look of love and gratitude to her father. He always knew the right thing to say. Not that her mother would listen, of course.

The large, now red-faced woman, opened her mouth to spew more hatred at her daughter. Before she could utter a word, the waitress came over with the food. The foursome again fell into a awkward silence and ate.

Not one more word was spoken at the table. They got up, her father paid the bill, and they walked to the car. They drove back to Katrina's house without speaking.

I'm going to need a fucking Xanax if this goes on much longer! Lisa thought. This was another first for her. She had never watched someone she cared about so deeply be hurt so much, without being able to do anything about it.

Her father pulled into the driveway and turned off the car.

Mildred broke the silence. "Kitty, we're going to go to the hotel. It was a long drive here and we're very tired."

"You aren't going to stay with me? The guest room is where you always stay."

"Not this time, dear. We'll be back tomorrow. We would like to talk to you—alone." With that, she shot Lisa daggers.

Lisa could take no more. She flung her door open, and deftly slid out of the seat of the large Oldsmobile. She ran around to the side where her beauty was sitting, opened her door and practically pulled her out of the car. Lisa slammed the door and ushered the now shaking woman into the house.

Katrina collapsed into a shaking, sobbing heap on the couch. Lisa had no clue what to do, so she went and held her head in her lap. The sobs and gasps went on for quite some time. Just when the time between gasps would lengthen, she seemed to start all over again.

The broken-hearted woman finally was able to lift her tear-streaked head and look the woman of her dreams in the face.

"I'm so sorry," she managed in between sobs. "That wasn't how I thought it would go. She's so hateful!" And the tears started again. She laid her head back down to hide her sorrow.

Lisa scooped her hand under that delicate chin and lifted her face to once again look into her swollen, magnificent eyes. "Why are you apologizing? You have nothing to do with how your mother behaves. I love you, and nothing she says or does will change that. Do you understand?"

Katrina nodded meekly, but didn't put her head back down. She instead sat up and kissed Lisa's cheek, then wrapped her arms around her and held her as tight as she had held her hand in the car.

"Have you been working out? Seriously, you almost broke my hand in the car, and now you're trying to squeeze the breath out of me," Lisa teased.

Katrina smiled through her tears, then started to laugh. At first it was a giggle, then a chuckle, then a full on belly laugh. It was contagious. Lisa wasn't sure why it was so funny, but she couldn't keep herself from laughing. The deep chortle coming from this slight woman was enough to make anyone join in.

In that moment, Lisa knew she would never love another woman.

That night Lisa went to her own place, even though that was the last thing she wanted to do. She didn't want to be there when Katrina's parents returned. She may not be great at figuring most people out, but it was crystal clear that they didn't like her. She also knew that she could've been the most charming person in the world, and they still wouldn't like her. It was very clear to her why Katrina had denied herself for so long.

Lisa wanted to be there to protect the love of her life, but she also knew her presence would only make things worse.

The next morning, Katrina told Frank she would be working from home so she could talk with her parents. She wasn't sure why she was doing this; she knew what they were going to say. She didn't care if they were not happy about her relationship. She was happy. She was in love. She felt complete for the first time in her entire life.

Her parents were at the door promptly at 8 am. Katrina had a pot of coffee going, hoping the caffeine would lessen the tension, even a little bit. She ushered them into the kitchen and offered the steely pair cups of black perfection. They took them and sat down at the table. *Well, that's a good start*, she thought optimistically. She poured herself one as well and joined them at the table.

Her mother stared at her with a piercing gaze. Katrina had her eyes, but that was the only similarity in their appearance. Her mother, Mildred, as wide as she was tall, now had salt and pepper hair, and bulldog jowls that jiggled when she talked. In her younger years, Mildred was quite striking. Years of anger and unhappiness had removed any trace of her beauty.

Katrina's father, on the other hand, was still a handsome man. Virgil had always been a slender man; age had not changed that. He didn't have much hair left, a few light wisps over his shiny cranium. His blue eyes sparkled all the time. He almost always had a playful smirk on his face. He was jovial, everyone in their small town knew and loved him.

"Well, Kitty," Mildred started, with the look of a woman who had just bit into a lemon. "I'm sure we don't have to tell you that we are not happy about you and this Lisa person. What will the people back home think? Do you know how this makes us look? They're probably going to kick us out of the church! We have been members there since before you were born!"

Her voice became more shrill with every word. "Did you even think about how this was going to affect everyone else? You need to stop this nonsense right now. I do not want you to see her ever again. Then, we can get everything back to normal. Maybe you need to come home with us. We can set you up with therapy through the church. They will heal you."

Her father kept his head bowed over his cup the whole time his wife was speaking. He was studying the coffee like his life depended on it.

"I will not leave my home!" Katrina shouted. "There is nothing wrong with me! I don't need to be fixed. I am happy. I have never been happy. I will not change anything to please you!"

Virgil finally picked his head up to look first at his daughter, and then at his wife. There was sadness in his eyes, a very unusual sight. He considered his words carefully before he opened his mouth.

"Kat, your mother is right. We fear for the sake of your soul. We only want what's best for you." He held her gaze.

"Daddy, what's best for me is what I am doing. I have always been gay. This is why I never told you. I would hope that you would want me to be happy, even if it's not how you envisioned it for me."

Virgil's blue eyes filled with tears. He once again bowed his head to study his coffee. Katrina shifted her attention to her mother. The expression on her face had not changed. She still looked like she could kill a house fly with a fleeting glance.

"I will pray for your soul, dear child," said her pious mother. She gulped down the rest of her coffee and headed for the door. Begrudgingly, Virgil followed behind her. The door opened and closed behind them, not another word was spoken by any of them.

Katrina was devastated, she went to her room and cried until she fell asleep.

She woke several hours later, dazed, she looked around, hoping it was all just a bad dream. She knew it wasn't. She loved her parents. They had been there for her her entire life. She was an only child, so she was always center stage. They supported her through all her crazy ideas, including the phase when she thought she wanted to be a lion tamer in the circus. They paid her way through college, so she could start her life debt free. She felt guilty for letting them down.

Lisa called that evening because she hadn't heard from Katrina all day. That hadn't happened since they met.

"Hey, love, everything okay?" Lisa asked cautiously.

"Yeah, just been a rough day. Would you mind taking a raincheck on dinner? I don't really feel like eating."

"Umm, sure. Whatever you need. I'll miss you. Let me know if you need anything."

"Of course, you'll be the first to know," Katrina managed a little laugh.

"I love you," Lisa said, not out of habit, but of true emotion.

"Love ya," Katrina quickly replied, then hung up the phone.

Ugh, what am I going to do? I love this woman, but my parents will never speak to me again if I continue this relationship.

She fell back against the pillows on her bed and, again, cried herself to sleep.

~9~

Katrina threw herself into her work. She felt if she stayed busy she wouldn't have time to think about her problems. She spent long hours at the office, barely speaking to Lisa. It hurt her heart terribly to do so. Her hope was that Lisa would get tired of waiting on her and just break up with her. That way, she wouldn't have to be the bad guy.

But, Lisa didn't break up with her. She gave Katrina the space she was asking for. She sent her flowers at work, just to let her know her feelings for her had not changed. Lisa was hopeful that all of this would pass, and everything would get back to normal. She had a long time to hope.

Noticing that she was getting a little shaggy on top, Lisa went to Sandy's shop. She didn't have to make appointments anymore, Sandy always made room for her favorite customer. She wasn't busy, unless catching up on the latest US Magazine is considered busy.

"You look like shit, babe. And I am not just talking about your hair. Come, let's hear it," Sandy said, patting the chair.

Lisa was relieved to see a friendly face. She didn't realize how much she had missed other people. Sure, she had her employees and customers, but it wasn't the same.

"I bagged the straight girl," she started.

"Well, that should make you happy, not mopey. Why so sad?"

"Her overly-religious, conservative parents do not approve. Since they told her they thought she was going to hell, I've barely even talked to her."

"I guess it's time to move on," Sandy suggested, as she skillfully welded her scissors over the bush of hair on Lisa's head.

"That's just it. I don't want to. This is the woman for me. I feel complete when I am with her. It's not even about the sex, even though that is amazing. She is perfect in every way. From her laugh to the way her face lights up when she eats scrambled eggs. I can't live without her." Lisa was close to tears, just thinking about all the things she missed.

"Well, then it will work out. Things that are meant to be always do. It may just take some time. Not everyone is lucky enough to have parents who always knew, and accepted it."

"You're totally right!" Lisa felt better already. "We *will* be together. I just need to let her figure it out."

"Alright, now hold still so I can shave your neck. Next time, don't wait so long to come see me. It looks like wild rats took over back here."

Lisa had to laugh, she had no idea what the back of her head looked like. Sandy finished with her neck and removed the apron. Lisa paid her tab and hugged her friend. "Thanks for setting me straight."

"Girl, the only thing straight about you is your hair!" Sandy laughed, waving goodbye.

Lisa left the shop feeling ten pounds lighter. Everything was going to be okay, she just knew it.

Weeks went by, they talked. It was very superficial.

Lisa never lost hope, though it was difficult at times She knew this was the woman that she was meant to share the rest of her life with. She had spent her whole life jumping from relationship to relationship, never having a fraction of the connection she did with Katrina. She gave her the space she needed to figure things out.

Whatever her parents said to her that morning had really messed with her head, Lisa knew that much. She was there, waiting for the love of her life to come back to her.

Katrina pined for Lisa. Every time she would feel her phone vibrate in her pocket, her heart would drop. She wanted nothing more than to be back in her arms. She was torn between having her parents in her life and having the unconditional love she experienced with Lisa.

She wasn't performing well at work. Frank noticed.

"Hey, kiddo," Frank said, sticking his head around her office door. "what's going on?"

"Just working on the Johnson proposal," Katrina said, distracted.

"That is not what I was talking about. I mean with you. You haven't been yourself for weeks. What's going on?" he repeated.

Katrina hated that he could read her like a book. "I'm good, buddy." She faked her best smile. "Just focusing on work."

"Alright, little lady. I worry about you. You have lost your spark. Tell Lisa to take you out for a nice dinner. You need a little break."

"I sure will," she said, not wiping the fake smile off her face. She hated lying to Frank. She just didn't know how to explain what was going on in her head and her heart. She actually went home early that night. Not that she really wanted to, her house was cold and lonely these days. She wanted to give the illusion that she had plans for the evening.

She drove home in a fog. She planned to put her sweatsuit on and eat ice cream until she couldn't breathe.

When she turned onto her block, she had to blink her eyes. She thought she was hallucinating. There was a black Oldsmobile in the driveway of her house. Her father's car. She flew down the block and into the driveway. She looked over into the old familiar car. There was no one inside. She jumped out of her Volvo and ran into the house.

"Mom? Dad?" she called out cautiously.

They were sitting at the kitchen table. They looked solemn until they saw her. Her father's face lit up, and he stood to wrap her into a warm hug.

Her mother smiled and said, "Hello, dear."

"What're you guys doing here? I didn't think I would ever see you again!" Katrina didn't know whether to be excited or angry. She settled for a mix of both.

"We brought you a surprise." Her mother's smile grew.

Katrina wasn't sure what was happening. She was cautiously optimistic. "A surprise?"

Her mother's smile couldn't get any bigger.

"Brock, come out here."

Brock? He was Katrina's ex-boyfriend. Her parents had always loved him. Katrina could never figure out why. A tall, dark, handsome man walked through the doorway.

Katrina's mouth went dry. She didn't know what to do. She hadn't seen Brock since she left her little hometown.

He was a good-looking man, she couldn't deny that. He had perfect wavy brown hair and brown eyes to match. He always had perfectly tanned skin, and he spent hours at the gym to maintain his almost overly-toned body. He smiled when he saw her, it was a genuine smile.

"Kat, your parents lied. You *are* more beautiful than the last time I saw you," he gushed.

She couldn't help herself, she blushed. It had been a while since anyone had given her such a compliment. Lately, she had only been told how tired she looked. "Thank you," she managed to squeak out. "What are you doing here?"

"I ran into your parents at the Walmart. They said the big city has not been very nice to you and you could use some company. So, here I am!" He grinned, and she couldn't help but grin back. "They also told me that there is an amazing restaurant just a few blocks away. I think you could use a good meal." He looked her up and down, noticing how thin she looked.

"Sure," she said, taken back by the whole situation. Her parents were in her house. She didn't think she would ever see them again. She was willing to do whatever it took to keep them in her life. "Just let me freshen up a little bit, I'll be out in five."

She turned toward her bedroom. She went into the master bathroom and turned the water on. She washed her face and threw on a clean white blouse and navy blue pants. She raked a brush through her long dark hair. She looked at herself in the mirror.

Whatever it takes, she told herself.

They went to Chez Michelle where her parents had made reservations. The food was amazing. Katrina ate her eggplant parmesan quickly. Brock watched her eat with what might have been a look of disgust on his face. Katrina didn't notice, she was engulfed in the taste of her incredible meal. She looked up at him once. He quickly turned his grimace into a grin.

"You must have been hungry," he said.

"I totally was! I didn't think I was hungry at all," she said, wiping her mouth with her napkin, a look of satisfaction on her face. "That was incredible."

"I noticed," Brock replied. "I'm glad you ate, you're looking a little skinny. You know I like it when you're a little thick."

"I know." She tried to hide her disdain for the way he spoke about her body. She thought her body was perfect, no matter how much she weighed. She knew she was beautiful.

"So how about we get out of here? Let's go back to your place, and I'll show you how much I have missed you," Brock said with a smirk.

She swallowed hard. She figured this was coming. *Fuck.*

"I think that's a great plan," she lied. Katrina was glad she had drunk a few glasses of wine with dinner, otherwise, she didn't think that she would be able to kiss him. Not to mention what he really wanted to do.

They got back to the house. The Oldsmobile was still in the driveway. *Whew! That will be my saving grace. We can't have sex with my parents in the house. That would just be weird,* Katrina thought with relief. Brock parked the car and headed toward the door.

What the fuck was that! He didn't even open my door! She couldn't believe the utter disregard he had for politeness. She opened her door and climbed out herself. She caught up with Brock and opened the door to the house.

The lights were all off, although the house wasn't quiet. The TV in the guest room was blaring. *Jesus, I feel like this is a setup. I guess I have to do this, it's what mom and dad want.*

She led him into the bedroom. He quickly undressed and flopped on top of the bed. Katrina knew what he wanted, so she slowly removed her own clothes.

Brock was never one for romance, let alone foreplay. She laid down next to him, he stroked her smooth breast a couple of times, kissed her nipple, and climbed on top of her. She wrapped her arms and legs around him out of instinct.

She laid there, making the noises she knew he wanted her to make. The whole time the only thing she could think about was getting it over with ... and Lisa.

She tried hard not to think about her. She couldn't help it. She had never had an orgasm with anyone else. Lisa could do little more than look at her to make her weak in the knees.

He finished and rolled over. He looked over at her and smiled. Then he quickly passed out. Katrina couldn't sleep. She felt sick about sleeping with him.

Not only was it possibly the most unsatisfying sex she had ever had, she realized how much she missed Lisa. She missed the way she smelled, the way she felt, the way she tasted. She missed snuggling after sex, falling sleep on her chest. She missed breakfast in the morning. She missed ... everything. She didn't sleep much that night. She tossed and turned between tortured dreams about Lisa.

In the morning she woke before Brock did. She quickly dressed and headed to the kitchen. Her parents were again sitting at the table, apparently waiting for her.

"How was your night, dear?" her mother asked with a knowing smile.

"It was good." Her fake smile was getting easier to muster. "Dinner was so good! I haven't had an appetite in a long time."

"I bet you have an appetite this morning too," her mother smirked.

Katrina blushed and headed to the coffee pot. She didn't want to talk about what happened last night. Not with her parents, not with anyone for that matter. They sat at the table, making small talk.

About an hour later, the bedroom door opened and out came Brock. He was only wearing a pair of sweats. Katrina couldn't deny that he was very handsome. He grossed her out all the same.

"Hey you," he said as he punched Katrina in the arm. He nodded at Virgil and kissed Mildred on the cheek. He helped himself to some coffee. "What's for breakfast? I'm starving!" He sat down next to Katrina and sipped his coffee loudly.

"I'll find something. I wasn't really expecting company," Katrina said, getting up from the table. That fake smile was now plastered on her face. She rummaged through the cabinets and refrigerator.

She found enough ingredients to make four omelettes. She chopped veggies and ham. She whisked the eggs and added everything to the pan. All the while, the threesome at the table talked like old friends.

She was annoyed by the jovial laughter behind her. She felt like a servant while the masters of the house lived the high life. She stuffed her feelings down, plastered her fake smile on and served her houseguests.

Brock finished his first. He let out a loud belch. "Thanks, babe. That hit the spot!" He smiled. His smile wasn't fake.

She smiled back. "I'm glad you liked it."

"So, Brock, did you tell Kitty the good news?" Mildred asked in a sickeningly sweet tone.

Katrina was confused. What news could there possibly be? She stared at him with a puzzled look on her face, waiting in sickened anticipation.

"I'm moving to Denver!" he exclaimed.

She continued to stare at him for what seemed like a very long time. In reality, it was a few seconds. *Everyone is excited. I guess I should act like I am too.*

"How is that possible?" She hoped no one noticed the crack in her voice which was caused by terror, rather than excitement.

"I'm starting a new job. My cousin started a construction company and hired me to start building apartment buildings. The pay is real good. And of course, I get to be close to you." He winked; it was almost charming.

"Wow!" she said. "When is that happening?"

"This weekend! Your parents were nice enough to help arrange everything. The moving truck will be here in a few hours. Your parents sure did a good job of keeping the secret. I have never seen you look more shocked."

Katrina swallowed hard. *Wait, moving truck?! He's not... He doesn't think... she couldn't even bear to finish the thought.* She had to sit down.

"Are you planning to move in with me?" She had to ask the question, even if she didn't really want to know the answer.

The grinning threesome burst out laughing. Katrina joined them, still unsure of what was going on.

"No, silly. I'm staying with my cousin for awhile. This place is too small for the both of us. We'll get something bigger, once I save up some money."

Katrina was able to squeeze out a few tight giggles. "Of course!" she said. "It is too small. What was I thinking?"

"Good thing you have a smart guy like me in your life, huh, babe? I'll help you out with stuff like that."

Her blood boiled. She hated being talked down to. Instead of expressing her feelings, she simply said, "That's true," and went back to cleaning up the breakfast mess. She scrubbed the pan for so long she could almost see her reflection in it.

Brock came up behind her and grabbed her by the waist. He held her against his bare chest and kissed the back of her head.

"I'm so glad that this all worked out. I have missed you." He sounded sincere. He was a simple guy, but Katrina knew that he really did care for her. She was going to have to figure out how to care about him. She was going to make this work—so her parents would be happy.

She turned to face him. "I missed you too." She was almost embarrassed by how easy she was able to lie to him.

The days went on. Brock was busy with his new job, so she didn't see him that often. He would come over a couple nights a week. Katrina would make dinner, they would have unfulfilling sex and he would go home. Katrina accepted that this was her life.

Her parents were extremely happy. They called her nearly every day. They would always ask how things were with Brock, and she would lie saying they were fantastic.

The more time went on, the more depressed Katrina became. She didn't notice, because that's where she had spent most of her life. It's very easy to be in a state of self-loathing when you're living a life that's not authentic.

Frank sure noticed, though. He watched as she started to dress in dark colors, she stopped wearing makeup and her work performance went down.

He knew what was going on, Katrina had told him she was back together with her ex-boyfriend. He also knew that her parents had orchestrated the whole thing. He didn't like what it was doing to his previously vibrant protégée, but he didn't feel it was his place to meddle in her personal life.

"Hey, pretty lady!" Frank said, sticking his head into her office. "I think it's about time you bring this boy around so I can give him the 'Frank stamp of approval'. Saturday night, let's all go to The Captain's Wharf."

"Oh no, Frank! Brock does not eat seafood. He says they're diseased little creatures. That God put them in the sea for a reason."

"Oooookkkkkkaaaayyyy, then what does he eat?" Frank was perplexed even further by this man.

"Burgers and fries, that's the best bet. He likes simple things. How about that burger place that just opened up on 42nd?"

"Joe's Burgers?"

"Yeah, that's the one."

"Alright, Joe's it is. Let's meet there, say seven o'clock?"

"Sounds good to me. Thanks, Frank." She gave him a sheepish smile, not the smile that lit up her whole face, that smile had not made an appearance in months.

Frank missed that smile. He missed the old Katrina who was excited about life. He said none of that; instead he gave a half smile and left the room.

Brock came over that night for dinner and bad sex. While they ate their three cheese ravioli, Katrina told him about their upcoming dinner date.

"Why would we have dinner with your boss? That's weird. What's his angle?" Brock asked suspiciously.

"There is no angle," she snapped. Then, she reminded herself to speak in a nice tone to him. *Brock may be simple, but he also has quite the temper when he feels disrespected.*

"He is like family to me. He is like an uncle. He looks out for me. We're very close." She hoped her explanation would appease him.

"Okay," he said begrudgingly. "I guess as long as he's paying, I'll eat."

"Good, I think you'll really like Frank and Marla. They're great people."

"Well, we'll see. Thanks for dinner. I'm going to go catch the rest of the game while you clean up. Let me know when you're done. Then we'll go to the bedroom so I can show you how much I care about you." He belched, then walked into the living room to switch on the television.

Katrina cleaned the kitchen slowly. She dreaded the sex more than anything. It made her feel dirty. She could convince herself pretending to care about him was okay. It was making everyone else happy. But the sex; it was even less satisfying than she remembered. It was always the same. He would climb on top of her and go to town until he got off. He would lie there for about five minutes, kiss her on the forehead, then get dressed and leave.

When everything was spotless, she walked into the living room to let him know she was ready. He was asleep. She was tempted to let him sleep, but she knew that wouldn't turn out well in the end. She shook him gently. He woke with a start and threw his arm back.

Katrina didn't have time to react and took the back of his fist right in the chest. For a second, she couldn't breathe. She panicked and fell to her knees, seeing stars.

He quickly jumped from the couch to her side. He picked her up and threw her onto the couch.

"I told you not do that! You scared me! I didn't mean to hit you!" he yelled. The yelling wasn't helping with the panic she was feeling.

She swallowed hard. "It's fine," she was able to whisper. She knew that he didn't mean to hurt her. She didn't want to make the situation worse by getting upset with him.

"If it's okay with you, I think I'm just going to go to bed," she told him when she was able to catch her breath and her vision came back into focus.

"No sex?" he asked, as if that was the strangest thing he had ever heard. "Sure, I'll see you Saturday." He kissed her on the forehead and left.

Katrina had never been so relieved to be hit before. It was a great excuse to get out of the thing she loathed the most in this farce of a relationship. She laid on the couch and the hot angry tears streaked down her cheeks. She laid there crying silently, until she fell asleep.

She didn't wake until the sun touched her face. She quickly looked at her phone. *Oh shit! I'm totally late!* she thought as she flew off the couch. No time for a shower! She ran to her room and pulled some clothes on. She rushed into the bathroom and raked a brush through her hair. She ran out the door.

She made it to the office in record time. She rushed into the office. Maggie, the receptionist, looked up when she heard her fling the door open.

"Good morning!" she smiled cheerfully. "Mr. Smalls is here for your appointment. I set him up in the conference room."

"Oh shit! I totally forgot about this meeting! Can you keep him distracted for ten minutes while I pull my head out of my ass?" Katrina pleaded.

"Of course! I'll bring him some donuts, he never says no to donuts." She smiled at Katrina and scooted off to the kitchen to retrieve the donuts she had brought that morning.

Katrina was so upset with herself. She had never been this disorganized in her entire life. She hadn't even finished her presentation.

She could wing it; she was good at thinking on her feet. She went into her office to calm down and grab her laptop.

She was lucky enough to catch her reflection in the window. She looked as bad as she felt. Her hair looked like rats had had a field day in there. She had mascara smeared under her eyes from crying the night before. She had been in such a hurry to leave, she had buttoned her cardigan wrong. She quickly put herself back together so that she was halfway presentable, and headed for the conference room.

The presentation didn't go well. In fact, in Katrina's opinion, it was a total bomb. She went to her office afterward, closed the door, and cried her eyes out. *What is wrong with me? That should have been a slam dunk. I just want to give up.* She cried until she felt like there were no more tears left.

A knock at the door.

"Kat?" It was Frank. Of course, it was Frank. He surely had heard from Mr. Smalls already. She opened the door.

"What the fuck happened?" he asked. He didn't sound mad, just very concerned.

She just started talking, she couldn't hold it in anymore. She told him everything, from ignoring Lisa's calls until she finally stopped trying, to Brock hitting her last night. He listened, his face becoming more drawn with every unthinkable word. It felt liberating to get this off her chest. She finally took a deep breath when she finished her horrible tale.

He looked into her eyes grimly. "Katrina. You have to stop this. Don't you see? This little charade is slowly killing you. You're not the girl I met two years ago. You're a sad, quiet shell. I miss my exuberant little bunny rabbit."

She looked horrified. "No, I can't. My parents are happy. They speak to me more now than they ever have. They love me."

"If they really loved you, they would want you to be happy."

"This is how it has to be, Frank," Katrina said with steely resolve. Another wave of panic spread over her. "You can't let him know I told you any of this at dinner tomorrow. Please."

The look in her eyes gave him no choice. "Of course, anything for you." He said it, even though every fiber of his being fought against it.

She relaxed, a little. "Thank you, Frank."

He gave his half smile, kissed her forehead and left her office. Katrina was exhausted. She knew she wasn't going to get anything done, so she went home early. She went straight from the front door to the bedroom. She was able to get her shoes off before she fell into the bed.

She slept until seven the next morning. She felt swollen. She was afraid to look in the mirror to see how swollen she actually was.

Instead, she made her way into the kitchen for a strong cup of coffee. She sat at the table, slowly sipping the black goodness. She just sat, her mind blank. She knew she had to continue with her new fake life—there were no other options.

She spent the day mindlessly watching Law and Order reruns. At about six o'clock, she decided she better get ready for dinner. She got into the shower. She didn't realize how bad she smelled, or how dirty she felt. When she got out, she finally felt brave enough to look into the mirror. She stood there, towel wrapped tightly around her. Her face looked much better then she expected.

It was her chest that she couldn't take her eyes off of. There was a large, deep purple bruise. She hadn't even noticed how sore the area was until that moment. She reached up to touch it, but stopped just before her fingers grazed it.

It was only an accident, she told herself. *He was startled. He was asleep, he didn't know what he was doing.*

She finished getting ready, willing herself not to think about the mark on her chest.

Brock rang the bell at exactly 6:45. He had showered as well. Katrina was happy about that. He had on a clean blue plaid shirt and dark blue jeans.

He smiled when he saw her. "You look nice." He bent to kiss her on the forehead.

"Thank you, you do as well." She smiled her polite false smile.

"Well, let's get going. I don't want to be late for our free dinner." He headed to his truck and climbed in.

Katrina locked the front door and joined him in the truck. They drove to the restaurant while Brock talked about work. He filled her in on the last two days at work and how much they had gotten done on the project, how two guys had just walked off the job, and what he had for lunch.

He didn't ask how her Friday had gone. She didn't expect him to, he never did. She had gotten used to being his audience.

They pulled up to Joe's. He paused to look at her. He thought, *She is beautiful. I am a lucky man.* He knew she was way out of his league. His saving grace was how much her parents liked him. He knew, as long as they continued to like him, she would continue to date him.

He squeezed her hand, then climbed out of the truck. He stood at the front of the truck, waiting for her to climb out and join him. They walked into the restaurant, a term which was an exaggeration considering the hole-in-the-wall appearance of the place.

The floor was sticky, the lighting was dim and the air smelled of grease. It was right up Brock's alley. Katrina, on the other hand, was a bit overdressed for her surroundings. She looked smoking hot in the black dress she had picked out. It had a high neck, to cover the purple monstrosity that covered her chest. It was knee length, although it had a long slit nearly to her hip. She had paired it with a pair of black boots.

When they walked in, every head turned. Every eye was on Katrina. She was the center of attention. Brock noticed. He didn't like the attention his date was attracting, it consumed him with jealousy.

"Maybe you should have worn jeans," he bent down to whisper in her ear.

She didn't respond. She almost enjoyed the attention. She had felt unlike herself for weeks. This reminded her that she was desirable. She smiled, almost her old smile. At least this one made it to her eyes before it faded away. Brock noticed.

Frank and Marla waltzed through the door. Frank's boisterous voice could be heard through the entire room. "Wow! Katrina! You sure clean up nice!" He grabbed her and squeezed her tightly.

Katrina laughed happily and hugged him back. "Frank, Marla, this is Brock."

"Nice to meet you," they chimed in unison. They all shook hands politely. Katrina could tell that Frank wasn't impressed, even though he did his best to hide it.

They sat at a table in the corner, it was a place where they could seat themselves. They chatted politely as they waited for their food.

"So, Brock," Marla started, "how did you meet the lovely Katrina?"

"We have known each other since junior high," he said, casting a quick glance in her direction. "Everyone

88

was in love with Kat. I was lucky enough for her to pay attention to me. Too bad I was dumb and messed it up the first time. Otherwise, we'd be settled down by now. We'd even have a couple of kids running around."

"How did you screw it up?" Frank was curious to the answer of that.

"I split her lip," Brock said without hesitation. "I got mad about something and socked her right in the mouth. That was the end, until Mildred and Virgil called, that is. They were the ones who got us back together."

Frank and Marla looked at him with the same perplexed look. Brock was at least observant enough to notice that. So he explained, "They called me. Told me how lonely Katrina was. They said something about her going down the wrong path. They set me up with a job with my cousin. Even paid for the moving truck. And, here I am."

Katrina was shocked. She had no idea her parents had set her up. Okay, she had an idea, but didn't want to believe that they would actually do such a thing. She could tell that Frank and Marla were just as shocked.

Katrina flagged down the waitress. "Can I get a double vodka on the rocks, please?"

"Right away, ma'am." said the very young blonde wearing a red plaid shirt and a very short denim skirt. This was the uniform in Joe's.

The more Katrina drank, the more she noticed how much she liked those redneck wet dream outfits. She also noticed how much Brock was liking them. She wasn't jealous at all.

Marla stood up after she had finished her after dinner coffee. "I need to head to the ladies room. Katrina, would you join me?"

"Yes! I definitely should do that!" Katrina jumped up from the table and grabbed Marla's arm, heading to the restroom.

When they got there, Marla turned and faced Katrina, holding her by the arms. "Katrina, I love you like you were my own child. So, think of that when I tell you this. You deserve to be happy. Stop spending your life making everyone else happy. This guy is a douche. You don't even like guys. You're in love with Lisa."

"No! I have to be with him! My parents won't speak to me if I'm gay! I have to be straight!" she cried.

The tears rolled down her face. She was pretty drunk, her emotions were raw. She looked at Marla with pleading eyes. She was desperate to keep this lie going. She felt like she needed her parents in her life, even if meant denying her own happiness.

Marla knew exactly what was going on in that fascinating brain. She softened, "Let's get you sobered up, dear."

Katrina nodded. They took care of business in the bathroom, then rejoined their table. The men looked up as they walked back to the table. Marla caught the attention of the scantily-clad waitress. She ordered them both a cup of coffee and a glass of water for Katrina.

Katrina was grateful to have someone care about her wellbeing the way Marla did. She agreed with her too, she felt very close to Marla, like family.

Katrina quickly drank down her water and coffee. She didn't realize how drunk she had been until she started to clear. She had been very upset. She thought drinking herself into oblivion would make her feel better. It hadn't. She felt even worse.

"I think I am ready to hit my bed," Katrina said, stretching. "Shall we call it a night?" She looked around the table, all three of the faces looking back at her looked relieved.

They all stood and headed for the door. It had been an awkward dinner. Brock didn't know how to join in on any conversation that had anything to do with anything except Katrina or football. He had barely graduated high school and felt intimidated around people like Frank, who had multiple degrees.

Katrina climbed into the truck. They covered the few blocks to her house quickly. He pulled into the driveway and killed the engine. He turned to her. "How about I actually stay the night tonight?"

She saw the gleam in his eye. Her stomach turned. She couldn't tell if it was the vodka or the thought of what he expected when he got inside her house.

"I don't really feel up to it tonight," she said.

"I'm not taking no for an answer two times in a row." He jumped out of the truck. For the first time ever, he opened her door. It wasn't a chivalrous act. It was possessive. He grabbed her by the arm and lead her inside. He took her to the bedroom and told her to undress. Obediently, she did as she was told.

"Lay on the bed," he ordered. She did. He took his clothes off. He laid his body on top of hers. He kissed her deeply, tongue thrusting to the back of her throat. Then he entered her, grunting until he reached climax.

Katrina, all the while, made the noises she was supposed to make, arched her back at the expected times, and was completely unfulfilled.

Brock quickly fell asleep after he rolled off her. Katrina, of course, was now wide awake. She blamed the coffee that she drank after dinner, though she knew the real reason.

She laid there most of the night, listened to him snore, quietly sobbing. She felt more dirty and used that she ever had.

Is this worth a relationship with my parents? I am miserable. If my parents really love me, they'll understand why I don't want to be with Brock. I know they always thought we should have ended up together. I know that's why they brought him here. We may be able to give them perfect little grandchildren, but they'll be dumber than a box of rocks, if they take after him.

She definitely had some big decisions to make. She finally drifted off to sleep when the sun was coming up.

She woke to him shaking her. "Babe, wake up. I need coffee." he was saying.

Her eyes popped open, and she turned to look at him.

"Okay."

She got up, put some sweats on and headed to the kitchen. She silently made the coffee. She sat at the table to wait for the pot to finish.

Brock joined her at some point before it was done. He sat at the table and waited for her to bring him his cup. They sat in silence, sipping away. Katrina's head pounded. Brock didn't seem to notice her distress. She looked at him.

Before she knew what she was doing, she said, "I don't want to do this anymore. I don't love you. It's not fair to anyone to keep doing this."

"What are you saying?" he looked dumbfounded.

"I am breaking up with you."

"Are you crazy! I'm the best thing that has ever happened to you! I'm buying a house for us." The look on his face changed suddenly. "Fine, I'll go. But, you know you won't be able to stay away for long."

He got up and went to the bedroom to grab his stuff. He walked out holding his clothes. Out of habit, he went over and kissed her on the forehead and left.

Well, that was weird. If I had known he was going to take it that well, I would have done this a long time ago. She felt fifty pounds lighter. She gulped the rest of her coffee and headed to the shower.

For the first time in a long time, she had the energy to clean the house. She even turned on some music and danced while she was cleaning. She didn't stop until everything was spotless.

She sat down on the couch and her stomach growled. It was nearly six o'clock. She had not eaten all day. She decided to splurge a little and order a pizza.

About 30 minutes later, the doorbell rang. *Pizza!* She thought. She skipped to the door and flung it open. Instead of the pizza delivery person, there stood Brock. He was obviously drunk.

"Brock, what are you doing here?"

"Shut up." It was all he said as he roughly pushed her inside. "I talked to your parents. They said if you break up with me, they'll never talk to you again."

"That's how it has to be then."

"I don't think so," he said, pushing her down on the couch.

She hadn't been afraid until this moment. "What are you doing?" she asked, alarmed.

"Showing you that I am the man here." He slapped her across the face.

She cried out in pain and shock. His eyes flashed, he hit her again, this time with his fist.

She fell back against the arm of the couch. She could already feel her eye swelling. She knew her life was in danger; she searched her pocket for her phone. It wasn't there. It must have fallen out. She shoved her hands between the cushions of the couch. Her hand quickly felt the smooth screen of the phone. She pulled it out and had 911 dialed before he snatched it out of her hand and threw it across the room. She tried to get up; he pushed her down.

She looked at him, with terror in her eyes. He looked back at her with blank eyes, as if he wasn't really behind them. He hit her again. This time she felt her lip split open and gush blood.

"Please stop, Brock!" she pleaded.

"No!" he shouted back. "You should have thought about that this morning. I'm the man here," he said, pushing her to a lying position and ripping her pants off.

She fought him. It was no use. He was much bigger and stronger than her. She didn't give up. She kicked and screamed the whole time. She was screaming so loud, neither of them heard the doorbell.

He continued to punch her as he raped her. She never stopped fighting back and screaming. Just as he began to choke her and she felt the life start to drain out of her, there was a crash behind him.

Brock turned to face two uniformed officers with guns pointed at him. If he were in his right mind, he would have stopped. Instead, he squeezed harder. One of the officers moved forward quickly hitting him in the head with his baton.

Brock shook his head, a little stunned, but he didn't let go. The cops exchanged a look. The second officer came forward and tased Brock. That did it. He fell onto the coffee table, shattering it. He lay on the floor, twitching.

The officers immediately shifted their attention to Katrina. She was breathing, but no longer conscious.

The second officer grabbed his radio, "We need a bus to our location, now!"

~10~

The paramedics got there quickly, transporting her to the hospital in record time. The doctors knew she would need surgery to repair her broken eye socket.

The cops had found her purse, so they were able to identify her. She had been at the hospital a few years ago when she sprained her ankle during a 5k. They called her emergency contact.

Frank showed up in record time. He was terrified; the doctors wouldn't tell him anything over the phone.

"Is she okay?" he frantically asked the first doctor he found.

The doctor ushered him into a private room and gestured for him to sit in the chair across from him.

"She is going to be okay. She took quite a beating. She is lucky the pizza delivery boy called us. Otherwise, this would be a different conversation. She needs surgery to repair a broken eye socket."

"Can I see her?" Frank asked with desperation born of concern.

"Sure, you can go in for a few moments before we take her to surgery. She has been awake on and off. I must warn you, she looks pretty bad at this point."

Frank nodded and followed the doctor to the room Katrina was being treated in. She looked like hell. Blood covered her swollen, misshapen face. There was a large bruise around her neck.

He rushed to her. She opened her right eye. "What the hell happened?" he asked.

"I broke up with Brock. He didn't take it well." She attempted to smile, it came across as more of a grimace.

"Where is that son of a bitch? I'll fucking kill him!" his voice boomed.

The officer that was standing in the corner took a step forward. "You don't have to worry about him, sir. He's handcuffed to a bed down the hall. He won't hurt her again."

"Did you shoot him?"

The officer smiled. "No, sir. I tased him though. He'll be going to jail for a long time after they clear him medically. I'll personally book him in."

Frank reached out his hand. "Thank you, sir. You saved my girl's life."

"Just doing my job, sir." The officer shook his hand and smiled.

The doctor came in. "The operating room is ready. We need to move quickly to save the vision in that eye."

"Yes, of course." Frank turned to Katrina, looking for a place to kiss her. There was nowhere on her face that wasn't covered in blood. So he instead took her hand and squeezed. "Love you, kid."

"Love you too, Frank."

They rolled her out of the room and down the hall. Frank stood in the empty room for a few moments. He couldn't believe this had happened. He was good at reading people. He had just thought Brock was a dumb redneck, he didn't think he was capable of this level of violence.

In a trance, he made his way to the waiting room. Marla was waiting for him there. He filled her in on what had happened. She went pale. She was as shocked as Frank was. They sat in silence waiting for word from the operating room.

A few hours later, the doctor came back out. "Everything went well. We will not know how much vision she'll regain until the swelling goes down. She needs to stay in the hospital for a couple of days so we can monitor her. You can check with the nurses' station on the fifth floor to see what room they assigned to her."

Frank and Marla thanked the doctor. They headed to the elevators and to the fifth floor. The nurse pointed them to the room that Katrina would be staying in. They headed down the hall. Just as they reached the door, Marla stopped.

"I need to make a quick phone call, dear."

Frank nodded and went into the room to wait. Marla made her phone call, then joined her husband.

Thirty minutes later, Katrina was wheeled into the room. She looked slightly better. The left side of her face was bandaged, and the blood had been scrubbed off. She was sleepy from the anesthesia. Frank and Marla left after the nurse assured them she was in good hands and was stable.

Katrina woke a few hours later. She kept her eyes closed, she felt pretty foggy. She couldn't remember what had happened. And then, she did remember. She slowly touched the left side of her face. She ran her fingers over the bandages, tears rolled out of her right eye.

Someone gently took her hand. Katrina was relieved not to be alone. It took her a few minutes to question who's hand was holding hers. She was almost afraid to open her eye, but she had to know. She knew it wasn't Frank's rough mitt.

She turned her head and slowly opened her eye. Everything was blurry, she blinked her eye a few times to clear it. When her vision cleared, she thought she must be hallucinating.

"Hello Beautiful," Lisa whispered softly.

Katrina just stared. She didn't think she would ever see Lisa again. She remembered all the awful things she had done to Lisa to keep her away.

She began to cry again. "I'm so sorry! I don't know why you're even here! I treated you like shit!"

"Sssshhh, it doesn't matter. It's already forgotten. I love you," Lisa reassured her.

Katrina squeezed Lisa's hand. She looked at her through her one tear-blurred eye. *I don't deserve to be loved like this. She should never want to speak to me again.* She didn't say anything for a long time, she wasn't sure what to say.

"I love you too," she was finally able to say.

Lisa smiled. "Get some rest, you've had a hell of a day."

Katrina laughed. "That is the understatement of the year! Will you be here when I wake up?"

"I'll be in this exact spot." Lisa kissed her cheek. She didn't let go of Katrina's hand.

Lisa didn't sleep that night. She knew Brock would never be able to hurt Katrina again, that wasn't it. She felt that if she slept, she would awaken and realize this was a dream. She didn't want to lose Katrina again. The last few months were unbearable.

She knew Katrina was the love of her life. She would sometimes sit outside of Katrina's house at night, just so she could see her. She stopped two months ago when she saw Brock leave the house.

Her heart broke. She couldn't imagine Katrina with anyone else, let alone a man. It wasn't unexpected. It was obvious that her parents were not happy about the situation. She also knew how important her parents were to Katrina. She wasn't angry at all. And now, looking at this sleeping angel, none of that even mattered.

Early the next morning the surgeon came in to check on Katrina.

Lisa took his hand. "Thank you for taking care of my love."

He smiled. "The damage was pretty extensive. It will require quite a bit of time to heal. The good news is, she should have normal sight in that eye. The bad news is, she will have some scarring on that side of her face."

"She'll still be the most amazing woman in the world," Lisa responded.

Katrina stirred. She opened her eye to see the surgeon. She didn't remember him from yesterday.

The doctor could see the confusion on her face. "I'm Dr. Smithers. I'm the one that performed your surgery. I was just telling Lisa how things went. I'd like to remove the bandage and see how things are healing under there. Would that be alright with you?"

Katrina nodded nervously. She wasn't sure she wanted to see what was under there. She knew how it felt— huge, swollen, ugly. She watched while the doctor washed his hands and put on gloves.

He smiled down at her. He gently pulled the tape back to expose his handy work. He continued to smile.

"It looks good, Katrina. It is pretty swollen, that is to be expected. Can you see out of the left eye?" he asked after inspecting her face closely.

She closed her right eye. "I can see, it's a little blurry. But, I can see."

"That is great!" Dr. Smithers said. "I want you to hang out here for a day, so we can monitor you. As long as everything is still looking good tomorrow, you can go home."

She nodded. Lisa thanked him. Katrina focused on Lisa's face. She was trying to read it to see how awful she looked. Lisa continued to look at her the same as she had always looked at her, with adoration.

Finally, Katrina couldn't stand it anymore. "How bad is it?" she blurted out.

"It's not bad, Love. It is swollen and bruised. You're still the most magnificent woman I have ever laid my eyes on."

Katrina didn't believe her. "Help me get to the bathroom. I want to see for myself."

Lisa wanted to argue, but by the look on Katrina's face she knew it was futile.

They slowly made their way to the bathroom. Katrina gripped the sink with eyes closed. She was afraid to look, but she knew she had to see.

After a moment, she was able to gather enough courage to open her eyes. She looked at her reflection with shocked disbelief. The left side of his face was unrecognizable. The entire area was purple. And it was twice its normal size. She reached up to touch it. It stung when her hand grazed the skin. This made it a reality.

She began to scream. She didn't even recognize her own voice. She fell against Lisa and slid to the floor, still screaming. Lisa did the only thing she could do. She wrapped her arms around the horrified, shaking woman. She held her until the screaming subsided into angry sobs.

"Let's get you back to the bed," Lisa whispered in her ear.

Katrina nodded, but was unable to bear her own weight. Lisa scooped her up and carried her to the bed. She gently laid her down and climbed into the bed next to her so she could continue to hold her. They laid there until Katrina's breathing turned from gagged sobs to quivering gasps. Lisa propped herself up on an elbow and looked into her face.

Katrina closed her eyes. "How can you look at me? I'm hideous!"

"Open your eyes," Lisa said firmly. She waited for her to comply. When she did, Lisa continued, "You're the most beautiful woman in the world. Nothing will ever change that. Your face will heal. And I'll be right next to you every step of the way."

Katrina nodded. She wasn't sure what to say. She had no idea why Lisa would want to be with her. She not only treated her terribly, she was now hideous.

Before she could think of anything to say, there was a knock at the door. "Breakfast!" the nurse announced as she came in with a tray full of food.

~11~

The next day, the nurse came in. "Are you ready to go home?"

Katrina smiled weakly. She didn't want to go home. She didn't think she could go back there. She would always be reminded of what happened there. Lisa saw the apprehension in her face.

"You're coming home with me," Lisa assured her. Katrina relaxed. She felt safer already.

The nurse went through the discharge instructions with both of them, handed Lisa some prescriptions and wished them well.

Katrina looked at Lisa; Lisa smiled at her.

"It's going to be okay," Lisa said and kissed her softly.

Katrina believed her. She didn't know how or why, but she knew she was going to be okay. The CNA came in with the wheelchair to wheel her out to the car. She needed a little help to climb into the Jeep.

Her body was sore, not just her face. She was glad that she didn't remember everything that had happened, she remembered enough to cause her nightmares for the rest of her life.

When they pulled up to Lisa's house, she noticed Frank's truck parked in the street. She looked at Lisa. Lisa smiled, "I couldn't keep them away."

Marla and Frank met them in the driveway and walked into the house. "I went and got you some things from your house. I figured you would be staying here for awhile," Marla said, handing a large duffle bag to Lisa.

Frank squeezed Katrina, though not as tightly as he normally did. "I'm glad you're okay, kiddo. That son of a bitch will never come near you again."

"I brought over your favorite meal, eggplant parm. I figured you needed some real food after being in the hospital for a few days," Marla said.

"Just what the doctor ordered," Katrina quipped.

Marla went to work in the kitchen, setting the table and getting the meal ready. Katrina sat at the table and watched.

She realized these people were her family. They were the ones that were always there for her. They never judged her or tried to change her. She was finally coming to terms with the fact that her parents would most likely never be in her life. She was going to be okay with that. She had these three amazing people. That is all the family she needed.

"Alright, eat up young lady," Marla said.

Katrina had not realized how hungry she was until this moment. She dug in. It was painful to chew due to the swelling on the left side of her face. She didn't care. She relished every bite.

Lisa watched her eat. Even though she had been through so much in the last few days, she looked happy, peaceful even.

After the meal, the foursome sat and chatted for awhile. They talked as if they had not skipped a beat. Katrina was getting tired, however. Of course, Lisa noticed. They were still in tune just like they had been months ago.

"I think this fierce lady needs to head to bed," Lisa said, standing.

"I agree," Marla replied. "I'll clean up while you help her get settled."

Lisa helped Katrina up and guided her toward the bedroom. She dug into the bag Marla had so graciously packed to find something suitable for her to sleep in. When she didn't find anything, she went to her dresser to find an old t-shirt. She helped her change her clothes and climb into the bed.

Lisa kissed her on the right cheek. "I'll be just in the other room. If you need me, I'll be right here."

Katrina nodded and closed her sleepy eyes.

Lisa joined Marla and Frank in the now spotless kitchen. Marla had also found time to start a pot of coffee. Lisa sat down in a chair at the table, now realizing how exhausted she was. Marla brought her a large cup of black coffee. Lisa held the cup with both hands and sipped it gratefully. She looked up at the couple who had joined her at the table, they both had concerned looks on their faces.

"You look like death, dear," Marla said gravely.

"I haven't slept in two days," Lisa admitted. "I watched her sleep for two nights. I was afraid if I closed my eyes, she would be gone when I opened them again."

"I don't think you have to worry about losing her again," Frank said. "She was miserable without you. She'll probably never tell you, so I will. She hated that redneck piece of shit."

"It can't compare to how much I hate him. I know that he was just a pawn in her parents' weird game, and I was okay with it. But I will never be able to forgive him for what he did. She is the love of my life. And if I didn't believe in the justice system, he wouldn't exist."

"Don't you worry, dear. He'll get what is coming to him. We'll make sure of it. I have already been in contact with the district attorney. They have a very strong case against him, and they're going for the maximum penalty.

"Has Katrina heard from her parents?" Marla asked, remembering her own conversation with them after they had left the hospital that first night. It was weird. Her mother had sounded like a zombie when she had told her about the attack.

"Nothing. I obviously do not have their number. But, there has been nothing. And I haven't left her side, so I would know if they had made an effort," Lisa said with disgust.

"I'm not really surprised," Marla said. "Based on what I know, I wouldn't be shocked if they sided with Brock."

"I hate to agree with you, my wife. But I can see exactly that happening." Frank looked grim.

"We just need to protect her. Whatever happens, we'll be here for her." Lisa fell into thought. "They're going to want her to testify, aren't they?" It wasn't really a question. She knew the answer. Of course she would have to testify. She was the victim. Lisa hated that word. Katrina was too strong to be labeled with that word.

"We'll do whatever it takes," Frank echoed. "And it goes without saying, Katrina can take off as long as she needs. We all know she'll attempt to come back to work far before she is ready. It is up to you, Lisa, to keep her home until she is actually ready."

Lisa nodded. She knew that was going to be a challenge. She couldn't fail. Katrina would want to return to work quickly. Good thing she had an idea to lengthen her sick leave a little bit longer.

Marla stood. "We're leaving. You have a clean kitchen and plenty of leftovers for later. I know how Katrina can eat. And she'll need to eat to regain her strength. We know that you'll take excellent care of her. I also want you to take care of you. Get some rest while she is sleeping."

Lisa nodded again. She knew that this was an order, not a request. She walked the couple to the door, locking it behind them. She felt like she had the weight of the world on her shoulders. She did need some sleep.

Instead of joining Katrina in the bed, and risking disturbing her, she laid down on the couch. As soon as she closed her eyes, she was asleep. She slept a dreamless sleep.

An ear-piercing scream woke her. Lisa didn't even have her eyes open yet when she jumped off of the couch and sprinted to the bedroom. Katrina was sitting straight up in the bed, a look of terror on her face.

She must be dreaming, Lisa thought. She quickly moved to her side and held her. She whispered in her ear until she felt her relax a little.

Katrina's voice quivered, "I'm sorry. It was happening all over again. Please, stay with me." Her eyes pleaded for safety, comfort.

Lisa climbed into the bed silently. She guided Katrina back down to the pillows and held her as tightly to her chest as she could. Katrina's breath was quick and ragged. Lisa didn't relax her grip until Katrina's body had completely relaxed back to sleep.

The detectives, who Katrina didn't remember, came by the next day to ask some questions. In the hospital, Katrina was in no state to answer anything. Now, she was lucid.

"Hello Ms. Jones, I'm Detective Ruiz, and this is my partner, Detective Markus. We would like to ask you a few questions about what happened on Sunday, if that is alright with you?"

"Sure, I'll do my best." She gave the two men a weak smile. It still hurt to smile fully. And she was also painfully aware of how smiling made the left side of her face pucker. She sat at the table in Lisa's small kitchen, holding her hand as tightly as she possibly could.

"Can you walk us through the events of that night? Tell us every detail you can remember," Detective Ruiz requested.

Katrina told every bit of the story she could remember. She started with ordering the pizza and ended with when his hands were around her neck and her vision slowly going dark. She was astounded at how much she really remembered. Her entire body shook the entire time she told her story. She didn't make eye contact with anyone, but she didn't stop until the story was over.

"How long have you known this gentleman?" Detective Markus asked.

"I've known him since junior high school. We hadn't talked for years, but recently reconnected."

"Why would he attack you?"

"I decided I could no longer live a lie, just to make everyone else happy. So, I broke up with him that morning. When I opened the door, he smelled like he had taken a bath in beer. He didn't look like himself either, his eyes were blank. I think that was the scariest part."

Detective Ruiz was taken back, "Not the part where you almost died?"

Katrina laughed at the irony. It was close to her old happy laugh, but not quite. "I didn't know I was dying. So, that wasn't scary."

"Thank you, ma'am. I think we have enough, for now. We may be back with some follow-up questions. Here is my card. If you think of anything, or need anything, give me a call," Detective Ruiz said, handing her his business card.

"Thank you, detective. I definitely will." She shook both men's hands and Lisa showed them to the door.

After she had locked the door behind them, Lisa returned to the kitchen. She just stood in the doorway and stared at the stunning woman at the table.

She hadn't heard what had actually happened that night until now. She fell even more in love with Katrina in that moment, this was the strongest woman she had ever met. Katrina noticed her staring.

"What're you thinking?" Katrina asked.

"Let's go out to dinner. We have been in the hospital or here for days. I think some fresh air will do us both some good."

"But, my face," Katrina protested.

"Your face is lovely. We don't have to go anywhere fancy, just somewhere, anywhere you want to go."

"Mmmm, sushi sounds really good," Katrina blushed, her mouth was watering already.

"Sushi it is! Now, let's go get dressed."

They headed to the bedroom. Katrina found some suitable clothes in the duffle. *Bless Marla*, she thought, *she remembered the important things.* The bag was full of underpants and socks, a few pairs of pants and a couple of t-shirts.

Lisa escorted her to the Jeep and helped her climb in. They drove to the restaurant, laughing and talking the whole way. The place was a little hole in the wall, which was why it was Katrina's favorite.

They walked in, and Katrina felt like everyone was watching her, for a different reason this time. The hostess quickly greeted them.

"Oh, Katrina! We haven't seen you for long time! Come sit!" The excited Japanese woman said as she led them to the best table. "We take good care of you!"

Lisa smiled. It was endearing to see how everyone around her felt a connection with Katrina. They were lavished with the best sushi Lisa had ever had. They had easy-flowing conversation and Katrina almost seemed like herself.

As the last of the dishes were being cleared from their table, Lisa took Katrina's hands in hers and looked her square in the face. "I want to take you away. When you're healed and the doctor says it's okay. Let's go to Hawaii."

By now, Katrina knew that Lisa was serious. "That sounds amazing. Let's do that."

"Okay, six weeks is the standard healing time for most fractures. So I am going to book a trip for six weeks from today."

"Alright, that gives me something to look forward to, once I am past all of this." Katrina motioned to the left side of her face.

"For the last time, you're still perfect. Now, let's get out of here, so I can hold you until we both fall asleep."

Katrina couldn't argue with that. She stood from the table. She turned to leave, then turned back toward Lisa. It occurred to her in this moment that she had not shown any affection toward her in public. She wanted to rectify that.

She grabbed Lisa by both sides of her neck and kissed her until she lost her breath. When she pulled away, she wasn't the only one breathless. Lisa held out her hand, and they walked out of the restaurant together.

~12~

A few days later Katrina had convinced Lisa that she could be left alone. She felt guilty that Lisa was missing work for her.

Katrina was sitting in the living room of Lisa's home, reading a trashy magazine. Her cell phone rang. She didn't recognize the number, but it was local. Katrina answered with slight hesitation.

"Ms. Jones?" The voice on the other end asked.

"This is she. Who is calling?" Her heart was beating faster.

"This is Lieutenant DA Bushie, ma'am. I am calling to inform you that the arraignment hearing for Mr. Hershey is tomorrow. You do not have to be there. It is just a formality. The accused puts in a plea of guilty or not guilty and a trial date is set. It is completely up to you whether you attend or not. If he pleads not guilty, we'll need to set up a meeting so I can start putting my case together," he said.

"Oh, so he is going to plead not guilty?" she asked.

"Most of the time that's what happens. It's part of the deal. Don't worry, it's all by the book. And I am very confident in this case. I won't lose."

"Okay, that is good to know. Thank you." She hung up the phone in a daze. She sat there until Lisa came home.

Lisa rushed over to her, as soon as she walked in the door, seeing the weird look on her face. "What's wrong?"

"Nothing," Katrina shook her head. She had no idea how long she had been sitting there. "The arraignment hearing is tomorrow. I think I want to go."

"Absolutely, I'll be there with you." Lisa kissed her.

Katrina's face was slightly less swollen. She was able to smile with minimal pain. "Thank you. I couldn't do this without you."

"And you won't have to." Lisa pulled her to her feet and held her tightly. "I'll always be by your side. Even if you attempt to push me away again." She smiled and kissed Katrina's forehead.

"No more pushing," Katrina agreed. "I learned my lesson the last time." She gestured to the left side of her face.

"I'm guessing you're starving," Lisa quickly changed the subject.

"Always am! What do you have in mind?"

"I have some lovely steaks that are just dying to be grilled, some fresh asparagus and sweet potatoes."

Katrina lit up. She loved steak. She had to admit, there were not many foods that she didn't love.

She sat at the table and watched Lisa cook. Lisa was smiling and humming. She loved cooking for someone who appreciated food the way that Katrina did. She happily placed the heaping plates on the table.

Katrina had not taken any pain pills for days, so Lisa opened the bottle of pinot noir she had been saving for a special occasion. She couldn't think of anything more special than spending the evening with her love. She placed the glasses on the table and took her seat.

She raised her glass and said, "Cheers to the strongest and bravest woman in the entire world!"

Katrina blushed, but raised her glass. She sipped gingerly. The wine danced across her palate. It had been a long time since she'd had a glass of wine. Brock didn't like the way red wine temporarily stained her teeth pink.

"This is close to heaven," she whispered, closing her eyes and savoring another slow sip.

Lisa laughed. "Slow down, missy. You only get one glass."

Katrina stuck out her tongue, but dutifully put her glass down. She plunged her fork into the meal in front of her. She ate, relishing every bite. She didn't set down her fork, or utter a single word until every scrap of food was gone from her plate. She sat back in her chair after she was done, clutching her wine glass. She was satisfied.They sat and talked while she finished her glass. Her eyes grew heavy.

"Okay, love bug. It's off to bed for you. We have a big day tomorrow. I am just going to clean up, then I'll join you."

"Yes, baby," Katrina said, rising from the table and heading to the bedroom.

Lisa cleaned up the dishes, wiped down the counters and table, and corked the wine. She headed to the bedroom. It was her favorite time of day. She got to hold the love of her life while they both fell asleep.

She found that as long as she held her all night, Katrina didn't wake up screaming. Lisa didn't mind one bit. She would take any excuse to wrap her arms around her. She had missed out on it more than anything over the past few months. She vowed to never sleep another night away from her again.

Katrina came out of the bathroom, wearing only Lisa's t-shirt. They had not been back to Katrina's house to get more clothes yet. Lisa didn't care. It didn't really matter what she wore, she was always the most gorgeous woman in the world.

They climbed into bed, Lisa wrapped her arms around Katrina and kissed her deeply. They fell asleep intertwined.

~13~

The next morning, Lisa woke first. She took a few minutes just to enjoy lying in bed, breathing in the scent of her love, being excited to have another day with her. She slowly climbed out of bed so as not to disturb the sleeping beauty. Katrina stirred, feeling the intense gaze coming from her lover. Lisa quickly kissed her on the cheek.

"I'm going to start the coffee," Lisa said as she jumped out of the bed. She was doing her best to take care of Katrina. She wasn't sure how to make her feel better, other than to feed her and love her.

Katrina smiled, "Okay, my love. I'll be right there." She laid in the bed for a few more minutes. Her happiness quickly clouded when she remembered what was happening today. She didn't know if she could face Brock. After all, he did try to kill her the last time she saw him. She pulled herself out of the bed and joined Lisa in the kitchen.

Lisa was waiting with a cup of hot coffee. Katrina took it and kissed her deeply. "You know you don't have to take care of me?"

"I know I don't have to. I enjoy doing things for you," Lisa said as her cheeks turned slightly red. "Now, off to the shower, we need to be fashionably early."

"Yes, ma'am," Katrina joked as she rushed off to the shower. She wasn't sure what the appropriate thing to wear to an arraignment hearing was, so she picked out the one pair of black slacks she had and a purple button-up shirt. She really did need to go get more clothes; she just had not conjured up the courage to go back to her place yet.

Lisa came in as she was getting dressed to get in the shower herself. She had been very careful to let Katrina have her privacy. She refused to push anything on Katrina. She knew it would be a long time before Katrina could be comfortable being intimate physically, and she was okay with that.

Lisa quickly kissed her as they passed in the bathroom doorway. She knew how lucky she was to have her in her life again, she would make sure not to let her go.

When they were both ready to go, Lisa held onto Katrina's hand and led her to the Jeep. They drove to the courthouse in silence. Katrina was visibly more anxious with every block closer they got to the large stone building.

The only thing Lisa could do was to hold her hand and be there for her. They walked into the building quietly, going through the metal detectors one after the other.

They chose a seat right behind the prosecution table. They sat, facing forward, Katrina clenching Lisa's hand tightly. Lisa looked down to make sure her fingers were not turning blue. She wouldn't say anything, even if they were.

They had to sit through a few cases before Brock was brought in. He looked so defeated in his orange jumpsuit and shackles. He shuffled his way to the defendant's table, where his public defender was already standing.

It was that moment that Katrina noticed the older couple sitting behind his table. Her parents were there. She had not seen them come in, but there they were. They wouldn't look at her. Instead, they smiled at Brock. Mildred even blew him a kiss. Brock didn't smile. Instead, he flung a glance at Katrina.

"What are the charges?" the judge asked, snapping Katrina back into the moment.

"Attempted murder, first-degree sexual assault and aggravated assault."

"Alright, how does the defendant plead?"

All eyes were on Brock. He stood, head down, he didn't appear to hear the question.

"Mr. Hershey?" The judge said after waiting nearly a full minute for a response. Brock finally looked up. "How do you plead, young man?"

Brock cleared his throat, licked his lips, and took a deep breath. "Guilty, sir."

An audile gasp traveled across the courtroom.

"Do you understand what you're saying, son?"

"Yes, sir. I did all those things that they said I did. I'm not going to fight it."

"Alright, then. We'll reconvene in three weeks for sentencing," the judge said and banged his gavel. "Next case!"

The guards took Brock by each arm and guided him through the door that led back to his cell.

Katrina's parents sobbed quietly as they got up to leave. They still didn't look at Katrina.

Katrina sat in her seat, dazed. She didn't know how to feel about what just happened. She sat in stunned silence until the judge banged his gavel again. She jumped, startled out of her trance.

She looked into Lisa's eyes. "Let's get out of here."

Lisa nodded and helped Katrina to her feet. Lisa wasn't sure what to do or say. She couldn't believe that Katrina's parents took Brock's side. He had nearly beaten her to death; that should be enough for them to see what an awful person he really was.

~14~

Once they were safely back in the car, Lisa looked at her. "Where would you like to go?"

Katrina looked back and answered with little emotion, "The bar."

Lisa considered arguing with her, but saw by the look on her face that arguing was futile. She drove to the bar closest to her house. It was lunch time, so they were the only people there. They took two stools at the bar.

The bartender looked up from the magazine she was reading. "Y'all are early. What can I get you two ladies?"

"Tequila," Katrina said.

"Seltzer water for me." Lisa had a feeling she would need to stay sober for this one.

Katrina drank in silence. That is until she finished her forth shot.

"What in the fuck just happened? I mean seriously. He pled guilty? Like, that's it? And then, my parents. What the fuck was that? They didn't even look at me! What kind of monsters would choose the rapist over their daughter? And I almost gave up the love of my life to make them happy. The most judgmental assholes on the planet!" She stopped to take another shot.

Lisa smiled with relief. Katrina had said everything Lisa was thinking. "We still have to go back for sentencing. You have to give a statement."

"I'll give them a fucking statement. That motherfucker tried to kill me! He looked like some possessed monster. He would have killed me if the pizza guy hadn't shown up! That's my statement. He's a murderer."

Lisa knew she was right; she was sad that Katrina had been through all of this. "You tell them that!" she said. "You need to let the court know what he did to you."

"Oh, I will! Another, please."

Lisa had lost count of how many shots Katrina had drunk so far. She asked the bartender, "Do you guys have any food? I think she may need to eat something."

The pretty little blonde replied, "I'll grab you some pretzels."

Lisa smiled, at least it was something.

They sat at the bar most of the afternoon. Katrina eventually slowed down on the shots. Somehow, she seemed to transform into the old Katrina.

By the time it was five o'clock, it was pretty clear Katrina needed some real food. Lisa paid the tab and almost carried Katrina to the car. She drove around the corner to a greasy burger joint. Katrina devoured her double cheeseburger with fries. Lisa couldn't believe that was possible for her to look sexy with ketchup on her face, but there she was, as delightful as ever.

Katrina noticed her staring. Any other time, she would have been self-conscious. Instead, she giggled, "What're you staring at?"

"You have ketchup on your face, Beautiful." Lisa replied, carefully wiping the red stain from her lip.

"I'm a mess!"

"Yes, you are. Now, let's get you home. It's early, but I think it's time for bed."

Katrina yawned. "Okay, if you insist."

Somehow Lisa was able to get the still-intoxicated woman into the car and home safely. She got her into bed. She retrieved a bottle of water and some Tylenol, placing them on the table next to her. Katrina would definitely need that tomorrow.

Lisa climbed into bed next to her. Katrina was already asleep. Lisa, on the other hand, was wide awake. She couldn't stop thinking about the events of the day.

On the day of sentencing, Mildred and Virgil were most likely going to be there as well. She hated them for hurting the woman she loved, but she would never let Katrina know it.

The next morning, Katrina awoke with the worst headache of her life. She rolled over to see the water and Tylenol that were waiting for her. She smiled and took the pills into her mouth and washed them down. She laid back down and willed the room to stop spinning.

Lisa got up and made coffee. She didn't wait for Katrina to join her in the kitchen, she brought the coffee to her in bed. They stayed in bed most of the morning. By lunch time, Katrina felt good enough to make it to the couch. She remembered why she didn't drink like that any longer. It was a very non-productive day, unless cuddling could be counted as productive.

The next three weeks passed with little excitement. Well, other than the fact that Katrina returned to work. She started only working a couple of hours in the mornings.

Lisa and Frank wouldn't allow her to do any more. She insisted she was fine and needed to go back to work. They insisted harder that she needed to take it easy.

About a week into Katrina's stay, Lisa went over to her house to get more of her things. Katrina didn't think she could walk into that house. Not now, maybe not ever again. It was once her home, now she viewed it as the place where she was almost murdered.

When Lisa walked in, the sight took her breath away. Nothing had been cleaned up, the coffee table still lay in splinters on the floor, there was blood on the couch.

She walked quickly to the bedroom and shoved every piece of clothing she could get her hands on in the suitcase she had brought with her. She vowed to never let Katrina see her house like this. She would come over and clean everything up if Katrina ever felt the urge to come here again.

Lisa walked back in her own front door with the suitcase. Katrina lit up. She knew that she would have some more wearable clothes again. She felt more like herself already.

~15~

When the day came for the hearing, Katrina wasn't nervous, not even a little bit. She knew there was nothing to worry about anymore. Brock wouldn't be able to hurt her, or anyone else, ever again. She just had to go to let him know that she wasn't afraid.

She walked into the courtroom with her head held high. She sat in the front row with Lisa right by her side. They sat holding hands, not speaking, until the bailiff came in and asked everyone to rise. They complied.

Katrina couldn't help but to look over at her parents, who were also sitting in the front row, behind the defendant's table.

It wasn't unforeseen, nor did she care. They had made their choices, and she had made hers.

When the judge took his seat, Brock was brought into the courtroom. He shuffled in as best he could, the shackles not allowing him a full stride.

He looked devastated in the bright orange jumpsuit. The color made him look even more pale. He managed a quick wave to Mildred and Virgil before taking his place at the defendant's table.

The bailiff called out, "Court is now in session!"

The judge looked down at the pitiful young man. "Do you want to keep your guilty plea?"

Brock answered without looking up, "Yes, sir."

"Alright, then. You have been charged with attempted murder, first-degree sexual assault and aggravated assault. Before handing down your sentence, some people would like to say a few words." The judge nodded at Katrina and she stood.

She slowly walked to the microphone that was placed in front of the judge. She unfolded the paper with the words she had spent many hours perfecting. She stood there and read every word. Her voice didn't waver.

She told of how she had finally decided to break things off that fateful morning. She told how she opened the door, expecting to be greeted by a piping hot pizza. She told of the terrifying beating she received. And she told of how he had sexually assaulted her.

"I wouldn't be able to forgive myself if he was able to hurt anyone, ever again. That is why I am asking for the maximum penalty the law will allow. Thank you."

She folded her paper once again and walked back to her seat. Her heart was beating out of her chest; she wouldn't let anyone know. She kept her poise. As she sat back down next to Lisa, she looked into her love's eyes. They were filled with tears.

Lisa kissed her on her cheek. "You're so brave," she whispered in her ear.

Katrina smiled.

Next up to speak on Brock's behalf was Mildred. She talked about what a great young man he was, about the time he saved a young child from drowning in the river. How he always came over to their house on Sunday afternoons to watch football with Virgil after Katrina left home. How he was like a son to her.

After Mildred returned to her seat, the judge once again turned to Brock. "Young man, is there anything you would like to say on your own behalf?"

"No, sir."

"In that case, I am ready to hand down your sentence. I have reviewed all of the evidence of this case. I reviewed the medical records of the victim.

"Her injuries were severe enough to warrant surgery, son. She has a long road to recovery.

"The wounds on the outside may heal, however, the wounds on the inside are very slow. I want you to have some time to think about what you have done, and more importantly, why you did it.

"That's why I am sentencing you to 32 years in prison. You will not be eligible for parole until you have successfully served 20 of those years.

"That should give you plenty of time to think about your actions that night. You're lucky that you're still young enough to make amends and turn your life around."

With that, he banged his gavel. "Court is dismissed." He rose from his bench and swiftly exited the court room.

Mildred let out a wail, and flung herself over the divider to hug the newly-branded felon. He sobs filled the courtroom. Katrina and Lisa looked on in horror.

"It will be okay, Ma," Brock comforted her. "I'll be just fine. You'll come visit every week. It'll be like old times." The guards pried the prisoner out of her grasp, and lead him to his cell.

Virgil and Mildred turned and left the courtroom. They didn't even give a sideways glance at the two women as they walked past. Katrina and Lisa sat there until they heard the courtroom door open and close.

Katrina looked at the woman next to her. The person who had taught her the true meaning of love.

She kissed Lisa deeply. When the world felt like it had tipped on its axis, she slowly pulled away. "Let's go home," she whispered.

~16~

They didn't speak of the events of that day. They never did. They simply went on with life. Katrina worked as much as Frank and Lisa would allow. Her bruising and swelling slowly faded. She had nearly forgotten about the talk of Hawaii.

She came home from work one day, and there was an envelope on the table with her name on it. She opened it and inside were two plane tickets to Hawaii. One with her name and one with Lisa's. She turned to see Lisa standing in the doorway of the kitchen, smiling.

"I thought you forgot," Katrina said, slightly breathless.

"I made you a promise. I don't forget my promises. We leave a week from today."

Katrina was speechless. She knew it was the right time. She felt safe with Lisa, she knew she would never hurt her. She placed the tickets back on the table and took Lisa's hand. She led her to the bedroom. She turned to look into those amazing eyes. She could see the uncertainty.

"Please," was all she said.

That was enough for Lisa. She kissed her deeply, taking her time to savor every second. She wasn't sure she would ever be able to touch her in this way again. She slowly pulled her shirt over her head, taking time to kiss her smooth shoulders. She unclasped her bra, to expose her perfectly round breasts. She kissed every inch of her skin, softly, lovingly.

She carefully scooped her up and laid her on the bed. She slipped her skirt off and tossed it on the floor. It took every ounce of self-control she possessed to go slowly.

She quickly undressed herself and laid next to the most exquisite woman in the world.

She looked deeply into her eyes, searching for any doubt. When she found none, she continued. She slowly kissed her way down to her secret garden. She slowly kissed her a couple times. She could no longer control herself, she plunged her tongue and fingers into the sweetness.

She licked her juices until Katrina arched her back and let out a satisfied moan. She lay there, breathing deeply for a moment, her head spinning from the ecstasy. She climbed back up to lie next to the trembling woman. She held her until the shivers subsided.

Lisa pulled away to look Katrina in her eyes. She wanted to say so much, but she didn't know how, so she simply kissed her again.

Katrina laid her head on Lisa's still heaving chest. "I love you with every fiber of my being."

"I love you with every beat of my heart."

They stayed there, Lisa stroking her hair, for a long time. Until Katrina's stomach complained very loudly.

Lisa laughed, "I guess it's time to feed you. I have just the thing. You must get up and put some clothes on though."

"Are we going somewhere?"

"Only to the kitchen, Beautiful."

"Phew, I'll be right behind you then." Katrina smiled and kissed her before she got out of bed.

When Katrina was able to walk into the kitchen, she found the most amazing meal on the table. It was homemade lasagna, Caesar salad, fresh-baked bread, and a lovely red wine. Katrina's eyes lit up as she saw the glorious array of food. She sat down, like a child on Christmas Day, full of hope and wonder.

They ate and ate, as they had many times. They laughed and talked for hours. The wine slowly disappeared as they enjoyed each other's company.

It felt like this was how it had always been, like they had known each other longer than a few months. Like they had never been apart.

Katrina suddenly became serious. "I want to sell my house," she said.

Lisa was a little taken back. "Okay ... so what does that mean?"

"It means that I want to move in with you permanently." It was rare for her to be so forthcoming with her thoughts. Maybe it was the wine, maybe it was the amazing sex, maybe it was because she had almost died.

"Absolutely!" Lisa cried. It was impossible for her to hide her excitement that Katrina too wanted to make this permanent.

"It's settled then. When we get back from our trip, I'll get it ready to sell."

"No, you won't."

Katrina looked puzzled.

"You're not going back to that house. I don't want you to see what it looks like. I'll clean it up. I have some people I know that are great at those kinds of things. Don't worry, it will be perfect."

Katrina smiled. She wasn't worried. Everything would work out perfectly. "Let's get this mess cleaned up. I'm getting sleepy and would like nothing more than to snuggle with you while I fall asleep."

"That sounds amazing!" Lisa hopped up and cleaned the kitchen at record speed.

She nearly dragged Katrina to the bedroom. She had never been so excited to simply cuddle with someone. Every day there was another sign that this was the person she was meant to spend the rest of her life with.

They crawled into the cozy bed and pulled the covers up around their chins. Katrina lay her head on Lisa's chest, while Lisa wrapped her arms around Katrina. They were asleep within minutes of getting settled in. They didn't move from that position until the next morning.

Lisa stifled the urge to stretch, so as to not disturb Katrina. Katrina stirred anyway, almost as if she had felt the difference in the body next to her. She lifted her head to look into her face. They both smiled. It was Saturday again. They were able to spend a lazy day together.

Since Katrina had gotten hurt, Lisa had gotten help at the clinic, so she could take off as much time as she needed. Saturdays were part of the deal.

They spent most of the day snuggling on the couch. The only time they got up was to order Chinese food.

Katrina was slightly nervous when the bell rang. She hid behind the door. She relaxed when she heard the delivery man's thick Chinese accent. They ate right out of the containers, watching old Matlock reruns.

It was funny that two people who were barely old enough to remember Matlock had such a love for the show. Often, they would say the lines right along with the actors. Then turn to each other and laugh. These two people, who came from such different worlds, were similar in so many ways. It was like they had known each other long before they met.

That night they went to bed, without even changing out of the bedclothes from the night before. They were perfectly content crawling into bed and holding each other until sleep overtook them both.

They slept soundly, barely moving throughout the night. This was the new normal for them. As long as they slept intertwined, sleep was deep and peaceful.

The first few nights Katrina had been there, Lisa was trying to not force herself on her. Lisa slept on the couch, and let Katrina have the bed. Neither one of them slept well. It was only when they gave in to holding each other that they discovered what true peace felt like.

On one particular morning they decided they needed to actually get up and go to Sunday brunch. This was another new experience for the both of them.

They dressed in what some would consider their Sunday best and headed to Let's Brunch. This restaurant was only open for Sunday brunch. Katrina had always wondered how they made enough money to stay open, until they walked through the door. It was crowded with people.

Lisa was glad she had thought to make reservations. They were seated at a table in the back. It was less noisy in this spot, so they didn't have to yell to have a conversation. They enjoyed French toast and mimosas until they couldn't put another bite in their bellies.

Instead of driving home after their meal, Lisa made a slight detour. She drove to the parking lot where they had had their first dance. She put the Jeep in park and turned to the lovely woman in the passenger seat.

"Care to repeat history?" she asked.

"Absolutely! That is one of my favorite memories of all time!" Katrina cried.

Lisa started the music, then headed around the Jeep to open Katrina's door and help her down. They danced, holding each other close. It was even better than the first time. They had such a strong connection.

They didn't even notice the world around them. In that moment, they were the only two people in the entire world. The music stopped, they stopped moving but didn't let go of each other. This was home for both of them, and they both knew it. Nothing would ever tear them apart again.

~17~

The next few days went by quickly. Before the couple knew it, it was time to pack. They talked excitedly while they threw things into the suitcase. Katrina had never been to Hawaii, though Lisa had many years ago.

"Can we dive off of a waterfall? And go snorkeling? And zip line? And hike the volcano? And go to a Luau?" Katrina quizzed.

Lisa had to laugh. "Of course, my love. We can do it all. We'll be there for an entire week. There is plenty of time for everything."

For the first time in a long time, Katrina had trouble sleeping. It wasn't the nightmares that kept her awake, it was the excitement of the new adventure that was awaiting her.

As soon as the alarm went off, she was up. She ran to the kitchen to start the coffee and jumped in the shower while she waited. By the time she was out of the shower, Lisa was just pulling herself up in the bed.

"Get up!" Katrina cried. "It's time to head to paradise!"

Lisa smiled. "There's plenty of time."

"Whatever, go get in the shower, Pookie. I'll bring you coffee. In a to-go cup. Hurry, hurry!" She was only half-joking. She was ready to be on the beach already.

Lisa knew it was futile to argue, so she got out of bed and headed to the bathroom. Katrina didn't really need the coffee, she was high on excitement. She made a cup for herself all the same. She drank it while sitting on the bathroom counter, waiting for Lisa to finish in the shower.

She did her best not to rush her. She was so excited she was jumping out of her skin.

After what seemed like an eternity, Lisa was ready. She loaded up the Jeep and walked around to open Katrina's door for her. Katrina hopped in. Lisa walked around the front of the Jeep and climbed in. She looked over at Katrina. She had never seen her like this, like a kid on Christmas morning.

Lisa laughed. "I'm glad I'm the one driving. We would be sure to get a hefty speeding ticket if it were up to you."

Katrina could only laugh along with her.

They did make it to the airport in good time. Security was actually flowing nicely. They made it to their gate with an hour to spare. Katrina couldn't sit, she paced back and forth.

Lisa stood, watching her pace for about five minutes. "Let's go get some breakfast, perhaps a Bloody Mary too?"

Katrina lit up even more. "Yes! I'm starving. Let's eat!"

It never ceased to amaze Lisa how much Katrina could eat. They found a little restaurant, not far from their gate. Katrina was finally able to sit. Her motivation to eat was strong enough to get her to focus.

Katrina ate her Denver omelet happily as Lisa watched. Lisa loved to watch her eat, Katrina almost had a spiritual connection with food. It was a healthy relationship, so Lisa just sat back and enjoyed the show.

After they were done eating, Lisa asked, "Do you feel better now?"

"I felt amazing before!" Katrina replied. "I think a couple more Bloody Marys and I'll be able to sleep on the plane."

"Alright, we still have plenty of time before we board, so let's make that happen. Eight hours is a long time to be this hyped."

Katrina laughed, it was her old jolly laugh. "I'm just so excited to be going on this adventure. And to be doing it with my favorite person in the world. I might pee myself."

It was Lisa's turn to laugh. "Let's hope not," she said as she flagged down the waitress to order another round of drinks.

They sat drinking and talking until there were 20 minutes left before their flight took off. They never seemed to run out of things to talk about. They might have missed their flight they were so wrapped up in their conversation. Good thing Katrina was still excited enough to check her watch every few minutes.

They boarded the plane with just a few minutes to spare. They found their seats. Soon after they got settled into their seats, Katrina fell fast asleep.

Lisa's Bloody Mary plan had worked perfectly. If she slept on the plane, her internal clock would reset much quicker once they got to the island.

Lisa dozed as well, never fully falling asleep because she felt like she had to protect Katrina. They were surrounded by people they didn't know, so Lisa was extra protective.

Katrina slept until the tires hit the runway. Her eyes quickly flipped open, she realized what was happening and became excited all over again. Lisa looked over at her and smiled. Katrina grabbed both sides of her face and kissed her.

"This is the best day of my life!" Katrina squealed.

"The best day so far," Lisa corrected her.

"I don't know. It is going to be super hard to top this."

Lisa just smiled, she thought it would be pretty easy to top this.

They climbed off of the plane and were instantly greeted with the warm tropical air. Katrina closed her eyes and breathed deeply. She was falling in love with this place, and she had not even seen it yet.

They gathered their suitcases and made their way out of the airport. Lisa ordered an Uber and they waited. The sun shone on their faces.

Katrina smiled, Lisa smiled. This would be a vacation neither one of them would ever forget. The entire way to the hotel, Katrina pointed things out that she found fascinating.

"Are you going to do that the entire time we're here?" Lisa asked.

"Most likely, yes," Katrina said matter-of-factly.

Lisa tilted her head back and laughed. "I love you."

Katrina smiled, but was distracted by the sight of the beach. "Oooohhh, we need to go to the beach. Can we go after we put our stuff in the room?"

"Of course, I bet we can find some amazing food down by the beach, too."

Katrina's belly rumbled. "I forgot I was hungry until you mentioned food."

Lisa laughed again. Katrina's love of food was one of her most enduring qualities. There was nothing quite like watching her enjoy something with every fiber of her being.

They took their suitcases to the room. It wasn't just a room, Lisa had spared no expense. It was the most elegant room Katrina had ever seen. It had a balcony with French doors. The view was spectacular.

Katrina opened the doors and was instantly slapped in the face with the scent of the beach. She stood, closed her eyes and took in everything: the smell of the salt in the air, the feel of the humidity and the sound of the waves crashing against the shore.

She turned to Lisa. "This is heaven. Can we go down to the beach?"

"Yes, we can actually walk from here. I see a little pork stand from here. Let's eat and go dip our feet in the water."

Katrina could only nod vigorously. They headed down to the beach. The smell of smoked pork now filled the air. Katrina's belly rumbled again.

They got their food from the vendor, and went to find a spot to sit and enjoy it. Lisa had grabbed a towel from the hotel room. She spread it on the warm sand, close to where the waves were crashing. They sat and ate in silence, both enjoying the beauty of their environment.

After she finished her meal, Katrina laid her head in Lisa's lap. "This is the best day ever. Amazing food, amazing scenery, and the love of my life."

"Oh, honey. We're just getting started. This is going to be a vacation to remember."

"It is already a dream come true. I'm here with you." Katrina sat up and kissed her. A kiss reminiscent of that first kiss. Passionate, full of lust and love. Katrina mused about how much communication could be portrayed through a kiss.

Lisa pulled away and looked deep into her eyes. Everything that needed to be said between them was able to be said without a single spoken word. They both knew.

Lisa stood and held out her hand to help out the hottest woman on the beach. "Let's walk a little bit. I want to show you something."

Katrina had an inquisitive look, but didn't question Lisa. She only trusted fully. Lisa led her to a small tide pool. Since the tide was out they could see all kinds of little sea creatures through the crystal clear water. Katrina poked her fingers just below the surface of the water.

She was like a child, exploring this new world. She touched a starfish at the bottom of the pool.

She was startled at first by the realization that she had actually touched him. Then, she was excited to explore further. She ran her fingers over the rough tissue of the creature. She was entranced.

Next, she turned her attention to the urchin that was next to the starfish. It looked a little scary with its spikes. Katrina wasn't deterred. She touched it gingerly, enjoying every second of this experience. She was in heaven. Lisa just sat and watched Katrina exploring this little ecosystem.

They sat there for so long the waves began to lick against their backs. They stood and walked back up the beach. They held hands like they had always been together. They just walked, enjoying being together, talking about anything and everything.

"Let's go get some sleep," Lisa said after hours of walking and talking. "I have a big day planned for us tomorrow."

"I'm not sure if I can sleep! I want to take in every single thing Hawaii has to offer!"

"I'm sure you're more tired than you think. I have something in the room that I think will help you sleep." Lisa smiled.

Katrina smiled back. "Well, let's do it then!"

Lisa had had the nicest bottle of wine the hotel restaurant had to offer. She had instructed them to uncork the bottle and have it waiting.

Lisa poured the dark red liquid into two glasses. She handed one to Katrina and kept the other for herself. She raised her glass. "To the most memorable week of our lives."

Katrina raised her glass to meet Lisa's. They both drank deeply, smiling.

The next day, they got up and ate a large breakfast, and then headed out to their first adventure.

They made their way to a little shack on the beach. It looked like if you looked at it wrong, it would fall over. There was a little old man inside, he looked to be as old as the shack he was standing in. He smiled as the pair approached. "How can I help you?" he asked politely.

"We're going snorkeling this morning," Lisa replied.

"Aaahh, yes. You must be Lisa. The boat is ready for you. They will give you all the instructions you need on the boat. It is the first boat on the dock, right behind my office."

"Thank you," Lisa said and they headed in the direction the old man pointed. She looked at Katrina. She was afraid her love's face might break, she was smiling so big. She also wasn't really walking, it was more of a hop-skip combination. "Are you alright?"

"I'm better than alright! I might die from how excited I am at this moment. I have always wanted to do this!" Katrina screeched.

"Welcome aboard!" the blond and very tanned tour guide said as they made it to the boat. "Lisa and Katrina, I presume. Let's get this party started, shall we?"

Katrina hopped right into the boat. She was going to have a hard time sitting for the 15 minute boat ride. Lisa was right behind her.

Her enthusiasm was contagious. They chatted with the guide during their trip out to sea, he went through all the safety tips, and they felt prepared when the boat came to a stop.

"Alright," he said. "I'm going to jump in the water first, check everything out. When I make sure we're good, you can join me."

The two women quickly put on their gear, so they'd be ready as soon as he said they could take the plunge.

They waited anxiously while he surveyed the area. He popped his head up and gave the all clear signal. They looked at each other, grasped hands, and jumped together.

They swam for an hour, though it felt like five minutes. The guide pointed things out to them as they swam. Even with the snorkel in her mouth, Katrina would still squeal with delight when she saw something new.

Once they got back to the boat, Katrina talked excitedly about everything they had just seen. Lisa joined in, she loved the energy she was feeling. She felt an even more intense connection with Katrina as well.

The rest of the week was full of adventures. They took a bike ride up the volcano one day. They zip lined through the forest. They took surfing lessons and a helicopter tour of the islands.

One thing they hadn't done yet was go to a Luau. Lisa had saved this for their last night on the island.

~18~

They went shopping that day to get some Luau outfits. Katrina found a dress with large red flowers. Lisa got a traditional Hawaiian shirt, with blue flowers and khaki shorts.

They had to head to the hotel to shower and put on their new clothes before heading to the Luau. Their adventures throughout the week had worn them both out a bit. The shower helped to revitalize the pair.

They walked up to the area where the festivities would soon begin, they were a little early.

Lisa was the anxious one this time. She had been looking forward to this night since she started planning this trip. She felt like she may just climb out of her skin.

"Are you okay?" Katrina asked. She had never seen Lisa like this before.

"Peachy keen, Jellybean," She replied and kissed her on the cheek.

They took their seats at the table right up front. By now, more guests where arriving. Katrina watched them all walk in. Everyone seemed so happy. They had the same look of awe that she did.

"Can you smell the pig cooking?" Lisa asked.

Katrina snapped her attention back to Lisa. "Of course I can! Did you forget who you were talking to?" She smiled her infectious smile.

"Most certainly not! The most hungry woman in the world! So, until that is ready, we should at least have a drink to celebrate our last night on the island."

Katrina suddenly looked sad. "I don't want to believe it's over. It has been such an amazing week. We have had more adventures in this one week than I have had in my entire life."

"Then no sad faces. We've had a great time and made so many memories together. We're only getting started, too. We'll have many more adventures in this lifetime. Life is too short not do everything we want to do, right?"

"I couldn't agree more. That's one thing I have learned over this last year. You never know when it's going to be over, so just go for it," Katrina replied.

Just then the server came along with their drinks. Lisa raised her glass, "To adventure!"

"To adventure!" Katrina echoed and clinked her glass to Lisa's.

They chatted and laughed until the dinner was served. Katrina was extra hungry this week. She wasn't sure if it was from all the activity or from the fact that they were surrounded by amazing food. She decided it was most likely both. She ate as slowly as she could, enjoying every bite, knowing this was her last dinner in paradise.

After everyone was done eating, the drums started to pound. The dancers came out and put on an extraordinary show. Katrina and Lisa sat at the edge of their seats, taking in every second. The drumming came to an abrupt stop. For a moment, Katrina thought the show was over.

The MC came out on the stage. "Give these lovely ladies a hand!" he shouted into the microphone. When the applause had died down, he began talking again. "At this time, we would like to bring up a couple of guests to learn a little belly dancing!"

The crowd went crazy, everyone was clamoring to be chosen. The spotlight fell on Lisa and Katrina's table. They looked at each other, stunned.

"Looks like we have our winners! Come on up here, ladies!" The crowd cheered as they made their way up to the stage.

"Hello, ladies. Tell everyone your names and where you're from."

He pointed the microphone at Lisa. "I'm Lisa, this is Katrina. We're from Denver."

"Give them some noise, everyone! They're going to attempt to learn the welcome dance. Let's see how they do!"

The drums started once again. They followed the lead of the charming women in their grass skirts. They laughed and danced the best they could. They were nowhere close to as graceful as the professionals, but they didn't care one bit. They were having the time of their lives. When the drums came to a stop, the crowd cheered. They smiled and bowed along with their teachers.

"Would you like to say anything to your adoring fans?" The MC was back on the stage with his microphone in Lisa's face.

"I would actually like to say something, if that's okay?" Lisa said, her voice cracking. Katrina seemed not to notice.

"The floor is yours, my dear." He handed her the microphone and took a step back.

"I want to say quickly, thank you everyone for your support of our dancing. That was super fun."

A roar came out of the crowd once again. When they quieted, she continued, now facing Katrina.

"Katrina, you're the most magnificent woman on this planet. I knew that from the first day I met you. Not just on the outside, either. You have the most sublime soul I have ever had the privilege of knowing. You have inner strength unmatched by anyone.

"Most people would give up and hide after you have been through. Not you. You went into that courtroom and didn't flinch. You were unwavering. I already knew I loved you before that moment. But, it was that moment that made me know that there was no one else in the world for me. I want you by my side every day for the rest of my life.

"Katrina, will you be my adventure partner—my wife—for the rest of my life?" She knelt down on one knee and produced the most exquisite ring Katrina had ever seen.

Katrina felt like she was dreaming. Her head was spinning. She swallowed hard. She looked down into Lisa's eyes.

"Yes." It came out as a whisper. The tears in her eyes choked out her voice.

The only one that heard her response was Lisa. Lisa took the ring out of the box with shaky fingers and placed it on Katrina's ring finger. She stood and kissed her like her life depended on it.

The MC took the microphone back. "It looks like she said yes, ladies and gentlemen!"

The crowd roared even louder.

Lisa and Katrina didn't notice, they were lost in love. They finally separated. Katrina looked out at the crowd and held up her left hand.

ACKNOWLEDGEMENTS

Ms. Jane Leonard, who told me when I was in the 5th grade that I was a good writer.

My amazing daughter, Cloe, you are always there to remind me that I'm a badass.

Team 79 Unicorns, for your support to finish what I started. I couldn't have finished this project without every single one of you having my back.

Tracee Sioux for making this dream a reality. I am forever grateful for all your support to get this book published.

ABOUT THE AUTHOR

Amanda Wray lives in the Denver area with her wife, Stacy, and daughter, Cloe. She has written many short stories and poems. This is her debut novel. She works full-time as a nurse. She is an animal lover, as evidenced by her four cats, three dogs and two fish.

Get exclusive access to the next novel by visiting https://mailchi.mp/60d2b6ec0337/amandawray